Death in Distribution

The Eleventh STAC Mystery

David W Robinson

Discover us online:
www.crookedcatpublishing.com

Join us on facebook:
www.facebook.com/crookedcatpublishing

Tweet a photo of yourself holding
this book to **@crookedcatbooks**
and something nice will happen.

My thanks go firstly to Nicola Robinson, a former colleague, who gave me the idea.

And secondly to Paula Guy, who won the Crooked Cat competition to have herself included as a character in the tale.

The Author

David Robinson is a Yorkshireman living on the outskirts of Manchester, northwest England, with his wife and a crazy Jack Russell Terrier named Joe (because he looks like a Joe).

David writes in several genres but his mainstay is crime and mystery. In January 2012 Crooked Cat Publishing picked up the first of his popular Sanford 3rd Age Club Mysteries, The Filey Connection. Since then a further ten STAC Mysteries have been published by Crooked Cat, more titles are planned for 2013 and 2014.

He also produces darker, edgier thrillers, such as The Handshaker, The Deep Secret and Voices; titles which are aimed exclusively at an adult audience and which question perceptions of reality.

Visit the Sanford Third Age Club at stacmysteries.com.

The STAC Mystery series:
> The Filey Connection
> The I-Spy Murders
> A Halloween Homicide
> A Murder for Christmas
> Murder at the Murder Mystery Weekend
> My Deadly Valentine
> The Chocolate Egg Murders
> The Summer Wedding Murder
> Costa del Murder
> Christmas Crackers
> Death in Distribution

Other work:
> Voices
> The Handshaker
> The Deep Secret

Death in Distribution

The Eleventh STAC Mystery

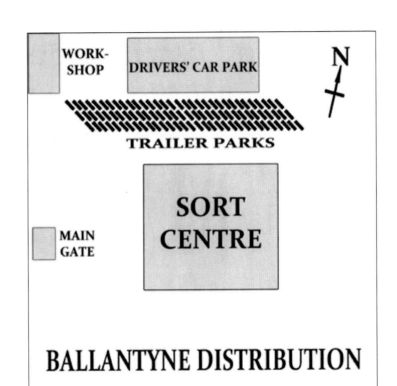

Chapter One

In an effort to put maximum stress on his words, Joe Murray laid his palms flat on the desk and growled, "The answer is still no."

Opposite him, safe behind his desk, Irwin Queenan, Chief Planning Officer for Sanford Borough Council, looked down at his gnarled hands. With no view through his window, other than the rear car park of Sanford Town Hall, it was easier to concentrate on fiddling with a silver-barrelled Schaeffer ballpoint than to look Joe in the eye.

As far as Joe was concerned, Queenan looked and acted every inch the local government officer. From the cut of his tailored, navy blue suit and his crisp white shirt, cleaved perfectly in two by a plain, grey tie, to the innate order and tidiness of his desk, the man gave out an aura of pointless organisation and assumed efficiency, which was not matched by any *actual* work, but which, from an administrative point of view, could not be faulted.

Down the several decades Joe had been running his café, he had had many arguments with the various Town Hall Departments, but this was the first time he could recall facing the *head* of any office.

Not that Queenan's rank cut any ice. Joe was no more intimidated by Chief Planning Officer than he would be a junior clerk on the reception desk.

Making an attempt to establish some control, Queenan declared, "Yours is the only business left on Britannia Parade. The Laundrette closed down last year, Toni's Hairdressing early in January, Dennis Walmsley's DIY store and Patel's minimarket closed last month. All those empty premises must be affecting your business."

"My trade is passing," Joe argued. "It doesn't matter to the draymen of Sanford Brewery or the truckers driving by whether I'm alone or in the middle of the High Street. All they're interested in is breakfast. And unlike the other traders, I don't rent my place, I own it. My old dad bought it just after the war. I am not selling, and that's that."

"You've been offered the market price, Mr Murray," said the third man in the office.

Sat alongside Queenan, Gerard Vaughan, the managing director of Gleason Holdings, shuffled in his seat. About forty years of age, the cut of his grey suit a marked improvement on Queenan's, the glint of a Rolex Oyster peeping out from behind pristine white cuffs and pearl cufflinks, everything about him said 'wealth'. When he and Joe had shaken hands, Joe noticed the finely manicured nails, and the soft skin, a stark contrast to Joe's own battered mitts. The man exuded an air of quiet confidence, manifest in his candid gaze and superior smile.

In the half hour since Joe had entered the office, Vaughan had said almost nothing, other than to introduce himself, but even when shaking hands Joe had taken an instant dislike to him, and his first contribution to the debate did nothing to assuage that feeling.

"This isn't about money," Joe retorted. "It's about business. Carrying on trading. What use is all that money to me? I've a good ten years to my pension, longer if the bloody government has its way, and I have no other skills than catering; feeding truckers and shoppers. And I live above the café."

"You've been offered alternative living accommodation." Queenan jumped in.

"A council flat on Leeds Road estate," Joe snapped.

"You've been offered alternative trading premises," Vaughan pointed out. "Help with relocation and setting up your business again. All of which my company is quite happy to finance."

"What you mean is, you're willing to abide by your legal obligations," Joe countered. "And the place you've offered me is on the other side of the road."

Vaughan picked a stray thread from his jacket sleeve. "Directly opposite your current location. So your customers will have to cross the road. If your places is as good as you say, where's the problem?"

Joe's contempt for him welled up and flooded over. "Do you actually know what you're talking about? I mean, have you seen the parade? Have you actually been there, seen its situation? Or did you just pick it out on Google Maps and think yeah, I'll knock that down?"

Spots of colour came to Vaughan's cheeks, his eyes narrowed and his brow furrowed. "For your information, I was born right here in Sanford."

"Yeah. On the east side."

"Like you, I inherited the business from my father."

"The difference being that your daddy was already a property developer, whereas my old man worked behind the same counter I do. Let me tell you something, Mr Sanford born and raised millionaire, Britannia Parade is a sort of layby off Doncaster Road. It's been like that since they made the road a dual carriageway. It's on the southbound side. The bulk of my trade comes from the north, the town centre area. The Brewery, van drivers from the engineering factories and smaller manufacturers. I get some from the industrial estate where you want to move me, and the rest are shoppers from Sanford Retail Park who don't want to pay an arm and a leg for a cup of tea and a bun. If I move to the northbound side, onto the industrial estate, like you want me to, I lose the draymen, the van drivers and truckers making for the motorway. They won't stop and cross the road, and even if they wanted to, once your builders move in, they'll have nowhere to park. Likewise, the shoppers, who don't mind coming to my place from the retail park, won't bother if they have to cross Doncaster Road. If I move to the industrial estate, I lose sixty to seventy percent of my business. That's hundreds of pounds *a day* I'll be losing."

Vaughan leaned forward and jabbed an irritated finger into the desk. "Right now, I'm losing anything up to a thousand pounds a day due to delays caused by your obstinacy."

"So it's all right for me, but not for you? Well, pardon me if I don't burst into tears."

With the look of a man determined not to be left out, Queenan pressed again, more forcefully this time. "Britannia Parade is an eyesore and it will be demolished."

"It's your development that will be an eyesore," Joe snapped. "The Parade was *built*. It wasn't thrown up in two months. The buildings were put up by craftsmen. They've lasted a hundred years or more. The crap you want to put in its place won't stand fifty. I am not selling and that's that."

"That is not that," Queenan assured him. "If you persist in your refusal, then we'll take out a compulsory purchase order on the property."

Joe had been expecting it. In fact, he had been surprised that Sanford Borough Council had not made the move earlier.

"Do you take me for a complete idiot, Queenan? Do you think that just because I cater for truckers that I don't do my homework? You go for your CPO and I'll tell you what will happen. I'll appeal. You know what that means don't you? You'll have to set up a public inquiry. Costs a damn fortune. And do you think I won't have the best barrister on the case? I can afford him or her. And it all adds to sonny Jim's delays." He jerked a thumb at Vaughan. "He'll pull in the legal bigwigs, too, but they'll cost him an arm and a leg, as well as his grand a day in delays. And it'll drag on for weeks and weeks. I'll make sure of that. Not only that, but I'll speak with Ian Lofthouse at the Gazette and see just how far we can drag your name," he pointed at Queenan, then swung his accusing finger onto Vaughan, "and yours, through the mud."

Queenan shook his head, let out a loud sigh of irritation,

and spun his chair so that he was facing the window, looking out onto warm, April sunshine.

Joe's gaze followed him. Like Queenan, he would prefer to be out of this stuffy office, and out there, enjoying the spring sunshine. He wanted to cut and run, back to his café on Doncaster Road, where he could be himself, laughing, joking and griping with the people he knew best. But he could not back down. He knew he would lose somewhere along the line, but if he was to secure the best deal possible for himself, for his crew, for his most loyal customers, he needed to stand his ground.

Vaughan put it into words. "You can call all the inquiries you want, Murray. You will lose. We will have that place demolished and more modern buildings put in place. As for my costs, well, I can bear them. A lot better than you can. Why not cut out now, while you're ahead?"

Joe steeled himself against the persuasive assurance in Vaughan's tones. "There is a way round all this, you know. A way in which we can all get what we want."

Queenan swung back to face him, his eyes suddenly alert. "Go on?"

"Something you've persistently refused even to discuss. Pay me what you're offering, but instead of leaving me on the industrial estate, let me have one of the new units you're putting up at an advantageous rent for, say, two years, just to re-establish myself. Do that and I'll sign right now."

Queenan shot a sideways glance at Vaughan who leaned back in his seat and shook his head.

"That won't be possible. We're putting up bespoke premises aimed at larger businesses than yours. Architects, solicitors, IT specialists, even," he smiled thinly, "business consultants. A truckers' café wouldn't sit too well in such a block."

"What you mean is, you wanna screw these people to the wall with exorbitant rents, and you don't want thirty tonne trucks spoiling the view... that's assuming you leave them

7

anywhere to park." Joe stood up. "No deal. I'm going to Blackpool with the Sanford 3rd Age Club for the weekend. I'm back Tuesday morning, and if all I hear from you by then is a compulsory purchase order, I'll be talking to my lawyers … and the Sanford Gazette. See y'around, losers."

***

Dave Kane, Transport Manager at Ballantyne Distribution, watched as Stan Crowther heaped a fifth teaspoon of sugar into his beaker of tea and stirred vigorously.

Kane had been with Ballantynes for almost thirty years, having started on the loading bays and gradually worked his way up to his present position. In that time he had been confronted with every conceivable problem, including personality clashes, but he had never come across an issue where the clash involved two employees from across the management/crew divide. He had been trying to find an amicable solution to it for the better part of ten years, and short of one of the two men leaving – voluntarily or otherwise – he could see no answer.

Alongside Kane was his number two, Peter Cruikshank, a slender and athletic man approaching his fiftieth birthday, and the target of Crowther's complaint. Cruikshank was the other end of this long-running and bitter battle, as tough, obdurate and resolute as Crowther, determined not to give way. He gave out an air of disinterest, which fooled no one, not least Kane. He knew what was coming, yet he remained outwardly confident of winning the argument.

Crowther was the same age as Cruikshank. Indeed, the pair had been in the army together, but where Cruikshank had kept up his fitness regime, Crowther had let it slip, and the result was a portly waist. Too much sugar and not enough exercise, Kane had long since diagnosed.

Sat beside Crowther was Amy Willows, union steward for

the drivers and traffic department staff. In her late forties, like Cruikshank, she had looked after herself, keeping herself fit, active, and slim, and her years acting as an arbiter between management and crew had not taken as much a toll on her as Kane's management position had on him, yet Kane suspected that she, too, was tired of this cat and mouse war of attrition between the two men. Still, she had to be seen to act on behalf of her member, and no amount of quiet words in Stan Crowther's ears would persuade him to back off.

Crowther sipped at his tea. "That's better. Got some taste to it, now." He put the cup down. "It's perfectly simple, Dave. It's Easter this coming weekend. I asked if I could have the weekend off, I was told I couldn't. I'd had Christmas off and to be fair to the other drivers, I had to work my Friday and Saturday schedules, and I'm due in Monday, too. Fair enough. I accept that. Last week, I asked if I could have an early start over the Easter weekend. Let me get finished at a reasonable time. I've got summat on this Friday and Saturday. The girls in the dispatch office told me to leave it with them." Crowther pointed a bony finger at Cruikshank. "Then he poked his nose in and gave me a half nine start, half six finish Friday, Saturday and Monday."

If Cruikshank was concerned, he didn't show it. He maintained that air of nonchalance which was his hallmark. "You got what was available. When I checked the schedules, half past nine in the morning was the earliest start I could find for you."

"Rubbish," Crowther sneered and gulped down more tea. "You saw it was me and made sure I got exactly the opposite of what I'd asked for."

Before either Kane or Cruikshank could speak, Amy said, "I checked the schedules, and it could have been arranged."

Again, Kane checked on his assistant, but Cruikshank still betrayed no other emotion than boredom.

"How?" Kane asked.

"We have a temp driver coming in to cover a four a.m. start. It runs Sunderland, to Middlesbrough, and back here. Then standby until three in the afternoon. My question is simple. Why are we using temporary labour to cover a premium shift like that, when we have a permanent crew member asking for an early start?"

Kane threw the question to his junior. "Peter?"

Cruikshank made a show of clearing his throat. "To begin with, arrangements with the temp agency were probably made over a month ago, and secondly, I didn't notice it. Today is Tuesday, and I don't know if we have enough time to change it."

While Crowther drank more tea, finishing off the cup, Amy wagged a disapproving index finger at both managers. "Three years ago, as part of a pay deal, you asked our members to be more flexible when it came to shift patterns. We agreed, and as far as I'm aware, there have been no problems. A part of that agreement was the use of temporary labour where shifts can't be covered for whatever reason, and we demanded that those temps must be as flexible as our drivers. Don't give us this, 'too late to change it' business, Peter. They're agency. They're temps. They don't work here, and when we invite them in, it should be on our terms, not theirs. If the agency in question is unwilling to alter their employees' working times, then go to another agency."

"And face penalty charges?" Cruikshank threw back.

Crowther put his cup down, and sat upright. "This is all hot air, the lot of it. It's because it's me. If it was anyone else, it'd be done, but because it's me, you decided it's not worth it."

For the first time, Cruikshank reacted, sitting forward, glaring. "If I wanted to get at you, Crowther, I'd be doing a lot more than spoil your Easter weekend."

Crowther half rose and peeled back the sleeves of his uniform jacket. "Any time you like, pal."

"That'll do, gentlemen," Kane intervened.

Amy placed a restraining hand on Crowther's arm and he sat

down again. "The ball is in the management court," she declared.

Kane had already made his decision, and he quickly rehearsed the correct phrasing. Although Crowther would get what he wanted, it was important to underline that he had not 'won'.

"Right. Peter, I want you to get onto the agency and change the shift for their man. Then tell the girls in Dispatch to put Stan's name in on the Sunderland, Middlesbrough job." He turned his attention to the driver. "Stan, you've got your early start on Friday and Saturday, but mark my words. I don't want you hanging out your time in Sunderland or Middlesbrough to make sure you can't be given anything else. I want you back here on schedule. And, you will be held on Standby until three at the earliest. Understood."

"I won't let you down, boss."

"Good. If there's nothing else, can we get on with our day's work?"

"I'm not leaving this here, Dave," Amy insisted.

Her announcement drew a sigh from the manager. "What do you mean, Amy?"

"I seem to spend most of my time settling arguments between Peter and Stan. It has to stop, and I'm going to put a stop to it one way or another. The first thing I'm going to do is get the union office to run a study on the way Peter treats the drivers. If I find any significant variation in the way he deals with Stan, then I'll be back, and I'm prepared to go to grievance if I have to."

"I treat everyone the same," Cruikshank argued.

"If that's true, you won't have anything to worry about then, will you?"

Kane readily understood Amy's tart response, but he could not let it pass without coming in to Cruikshank's defence. "While you're doing that, Amy, I'll have admin run a similar study, so that we're both singing from same hymn sheet. At the

11

same time, I'll get them to check on Stan's dealings with Peter, and if I find any variation between him and the other drivers, then *I* will be asking to see *you*." He allowed short pause to let the message sink in. "Now is that it? Can we please get back to work?"

With a few mutters and glares exchanged between the two men, Amy and Crowther left.

Kane waited for the door to close behind them before leaving his seat and crossing to the window of his third floor office. Behind him, Cruikshank waited in silence.

With views of Blackpool Pleasure Beach and Tower in the distance, the window overlooked the north yard, where the company trailers were parked at an angle which made life easier for drivers reversing into tight lanes. There were thirty lanes, and when they were full, they would accommodate three trailers each, parked nose to tail. Around the corner, in the east yard, there were forty more lanes, opposite the loading bays, each accommodating two trailers. Add to that sixty loading bays, all with a trailer backed on for either loading or unloading, and that came to 230 trailers in the vast yard. As an exercise in logistics, it was a mammoth operation, and for the most part it ran smoothly, without hitch … for the most part.

"It can't go on, Peter," Kane said.

He did not turn away, but continued looking out through the window, across the yard to the Maintenance workshop. Thanks to the design of the yard and the number of trailers parked there, coupled to an oversight in security, the third floor of the Sort Centre, was the only place where the entrance to Maintenance could be seen. From anywhere else, it was just another tall, broad building in the huge complex that was Ballantyne Mail Order's National Distribution Centre.

"Again, Dave?"

He sensed Peter moving to stand alongside him.

"You and Stan Crowther."

Kane looked again at the maintenance area, and spotted

several apprentices climbing into the wheelie bins. Because of its comparative invisibility, the crew of mechanics, tyre fitters, bodywork specialists, tended to play silly games which, Kane had often been at pains to point out, if they went wrong, could land the company in serious trouble with the Health & Safety Executive.

"Get onto Security, please, Peter. The lads in Maintenance are jousting in the bloody wheelie bins again."

He listened a moment while Peter rang the security office. When he heard the receiver replaced, Kane turned from the window.

"You and Stan Crowther," he repeated.

"Dave, I—"

Kane held up a hand to forestall the inevitable string of excuses. "I don't want to hear it. Amy may or may not carry out her threat to check the stats, but we all know the truth, Peter. Look, I retire in four years. You are my natural successor. You know what Ballantynes are like. They won't bring in an outsider if they have someone in their own ranks who can do the job. That's you, my friend. You know the company, you know how we operate. Who better to take over after me? But if Amy nails you for victimisation, even on the smallest of detail, you can forget it. It's personal, Peter, and you cannot be personal. You have to treat them all exactly the same."

"I hate Crowther," Cruikshank admitted. "And we all know why."

"I know, and I can't say I blame you, but leave it at home. Don't bring it to work with you. If you don't, if this business with Stan Crowther goes on, it's not him who'll suffer. It's you."

***

On the barren, stone staircase at the end of the building, a similar conversation was taking place between Amy and Crowther.

"It has to stop, Stan. One of these days, Peter will get something serious on you, and you will be out on your ear."

Only half listening to her lecture, when she had finished, Crowther pointed across the yard to the horseplay amongst the workshop apprentices. "That's where Cruikshank should be concentrating. Kids larking around like that. Never mind trying to do the dirty on me."

"And you're so innocent, are you?"

"I didn't start it."

"Yes you did," Amy argued.

Crowther faced her and shrugged. "What happened, happened. I can't make it un-happen."

"No, but you could be a bit more adult about it. All these years and you never even apologised. Instead you carry on making snide jokes about him behind his back. Try putting yourself in his place. What if it had been your wife and him?"

Crowther smiled. "I've never been married." When he saw that his effort to lighten the mood had no effect, he went back to sourness. "It takes two to tango, you know."

Chapter Two

Joe cleared his throat and read aloud from the letter in his hand.

"As you are aware, Britannia Parade, in which your premises are situated, has stood since the early 1900s, and Sanford Borough Council feel it no longer presents the correct image of a town looking ahead to the future. We therefore feel that the offer from Gleason Holdings should be accepted and that the parade should be demolished to make way for smarter, new, innovative business premises. In the light of your refusal to accept our offer, we are serving you with a Compulsory Purchase Order." He looked up at Sheila and Brenda, who sat behind him. "Any time you want something doing, like the potholes repairing in the roads, the council take months over it. The minute they want something done, like knocking down The Lazy Luncheonette, it happens in days. I only met with them on Monday, and I received this today. That rotten sod, Queenan, had the CPO in the pipeline before I turned up on Monday, but he didn't have the bottle to hand it to me then." He fumed for a moment. "And what in the name of bacon and egg sandwiches are innovative business premises? A building is a building, full stop."

"Never mind the iffy terminology," Sheila said. "What happens to The Lazy Luncheonette?"

"I just told you. It gets bulldozed," Joe said, "along with my flat, my living and your jobs. Oh, they're offering compensation and new premises on the industrial estate opposite, but there's no living accommodation with them, they're on the wrong side of Doncaster Road and I'll have to pay rent on it. I own The Lazy Luncheonette, but I'll end up renting a portakabin.

Combined with the rates, I'll be shelling out double what I'm paying now."

"Double?" Brenda looked down her nose at him.

"All right, about fifty percent more."

Sat in the jump seat, across the aisle from the bus driver, Joe had half turned to read the letter to his two employees. Now he turned again, to stare malevolently through the windscreen.

"Another twenty minutes, Joe," said Keith Lowry, the driver. "Give or take."

Joe responded with a taciturn grunt.

Overhead gantries warned drivers for North Blackpool to stay in the inside lane, and those for the Pleasure Beach and South and Central Blackpool to move to the right. Keith checked his mirror, indicated to pull out, and slowed down, waiting for a lorry to pass him. Glancing across and into Keith's mirror, Joe could see the side of the lorry making its way forward. His agile mind automatically translated the reversed wording on the sides as *Tyne Distribution*, but as the truck drew alongside and began to move ahead, he could see that more lettering had been erased, probably as a result of replacing a side panel.

Looking across the far side of the motorway and away to their right, bathed in April sunshine, Blackpool Tower stood stark against the flat, Lancashire landscape. One of the most recognisable landmarks in Great Britain, it symbolised the hedonism and freedom of the 'Fun Capital of the North', as the town was often designated, and until the arrival of the postman back in Sanford, Joe had anticipated a weekend of exactly that: fun.

The lorry drew alongside, and blocked his view of the tower. Half turning in his seat once more, so he could face his two closest friends, he said, "They've been threatening this for years. Britannia Parade doesn't sit well with those fancy shops in the retail park. So they decided to knock it down, kill off half a dozen small and profitable businesses, hype the rents on fancy new premises and no one will shop there because the prices will be too high."

"We know all this, Joe," Sheila replied, "but have you done anything about it? You know you can appeal against a CPO."

Joe grinned. "Already in hand. I rang my solicitor before we left this morning. Got him out of bed and told him to get on with it. If nothing else, it'll slow 'em down, while I think of something. Any idea what more I can do?"

"No point whining to your MP," Brenda observed. "He's all for it, and according to whisper, he's a consultant to Gleason Holdings."

Joe tutted. "Here I am asking what I can do, and you tell me what I shouldn't do." He took a breath. "Bloody MPs. And there was me thinking he's supposed to be for the people who voted him in. Y'know. Working people."

"Depends what century you're living in," Keith commented from the driver's seat. "And what would you know about working? You've never done a day's proper work in your life."

Falling silent again, watching the lorry slowly overtake them, Joe was acutely aware that the seventy or so members of the Sanford 3rd Age Club on the bus had their share of problems: health, money, relationships, and for those who still worked, the ever-present worry of employment security. He counted himself lucky. As the proprietor of a thriving trucker's café, he had no money or employment issues, his health troubles had drifted into the background since he gave up smoking, and any worries concerning relationships had disappeared on a plane to Tenerife when his ex-wife left him.

And now, suddenly, out of the blue, he did have employment worries. They wanted to pull down his café. The business, which had stood in the centre of Britannia Parade since just after the war, would be gone, and when the bulldozers moved in, they would carry off most of his trade too.

Keith's last comment resounded in his head. "Feeding idiot drivers like you is proper work," he argued. "At least, I don't just

17

sit on my backside all day, turning a steering wheel."

"You don't feed bus drivers, Joe. You feed truckers: dipsticks like this." He nodded at the passing lorry and checked his mirror again. "And I wish he'd get a bloody move on. I need to be in that lane."

"I feed draymen. It's not much different. They do just as much moaning and whining—"

The tail end of the lorry still had a yard or two to go when without warning, the driver moved to the left.

Shouting a curse, Keith braked hard and yanked the wheel to the left, steering the bus onto the hard shoulder. Cut off mid-sentence, Joe was flung from his seat to the floor where he struck his back on the front fascia. There was a clunk as the lorry clipped the bus and tore off the external mirror. Apparently oblivious to the collision, the driver allowed his vehicle to continue drifting left. Keith swerved further, ran over the drains on the extreme edge of the hard shoulder, and the front wheel dropped into a narrow ditch. Keith dragged the wheel hard right and pulled the front wheel out. The seventy passengers let out a chorus of cries, gasps, and "Oohs." Joe tried to drag himself upright, but with the bus swerving erratically and a line of cars ahead of him, Keith had to stand on the brakes, and pull the wheel right again, throwing Joe back to the floor. The back end slewed over and dropped into the shallow ditch, the coach tilted dangerously on its nearside before coming to a stop, and Joe rolled down to hit his head on the door.

Ahead of them, the lorry driver clipped more vehicles but still did not stop. The vehicle careened up the slip road to the roundabout where, without pausing, caused several vehicles to brake sharply as the driver pulled out and hurtled away towards Lytham St Annes.

Keith cut the engine, flipped off his seatbelt and crossed to Joe. "Are you all right?"

"Yeah, yeah. I'm okay."

Keith helped him up. "I'm sick of telling you to fasten your belt when you're on that jump seat. One of these days, you'll get me booked."

"Stop fussing. I told you, I'm all right." Joe rubbed the back of his head. "Just a bump on the nut. That's all."

Already struggling out of her seat into the lopsided aisle, Brenda commented, "A knock on the head like that can be dangerous, Joe. It might trick you into getting your wallet out."

"Thanks for your concern, Brenda. If you can, why don't you get along the bus and make sure everyone is all right." While Brenda struggled to leave the tilted seat, and made her way along the aisle, Joe concentrated on Keith again. "Did you get his number?"

"I don't talk to strange truckers."

"His registration number, you idiot."

"No. Did you?"

"I was busy rolling all over the floor."

"And I was busy trying to stop the bus from rolling over and killing someone."

"That makes a change from trying to kill them with your driving."

"Now listen you awkward old git, I—"

"Why don't you two stop arguing and get people off the bus?" Sheila interrupted, straining as Brenda had, to get into the aisle.

Joe stared. "Sheila, we're on the motorway. You can't have people wandering about on the hard shoulder."

"Shows how much you know," Keith said. "Sheila is right. You don't sit in a vehicle on the hard shoulder in case someone runs up your backside. As long as everyone is okay, get them off the bus and off the hard shoulder onto the grass verges." He took out his mobile. I'll bell the filth."

"The cops?" Joe protested. "I thought you only needed to call them when someone is injured."

"Joe, do I come to your café and tell you how to cook meat

pies?" Keith waved at his seat and the missing mirror beyond the windows. "I've no offside mirror, so I can't drive the bloody bus. And I don't know what other damage that barmpot trucker might have done. Now let me do my job, and you do yours. Get your crumblies off the bus."

While Keith dialled the police and waited for an answer, Joe took the PA mike from its rail above Sheila's seat, tapped the head to ensure it was working, and began speaking.

"All right, folks, as long as none of you are injured, I'm told that we have to get off the bus, then off the hard shoulder and onto the grass verges. If any of you have been hurt in the collision, let Brenda or Sheila know, and we'll make the necessary arrangements." He eyed Keith sourly. "As well as starting on the legal claims."

"What are we doing about getting to the hotel, Joe," Alec Staines asked from half way down on the offside.

"We can't do anything. According to our pilot, the bus can't be moved because he doesn't know the extent of the damage." Once again, he glanced sideways at Keith, now talking into his phone. "I'm sure the cops will arrange something."

"Did anyone get that idiot's registration?" Captain Tanner demanded.

"No, but we know which company he works for, Les. It won't take long to track him down."

Joe hooked the microphone back up, as Brenda and Sheila returned reporting that everyone was okay.

Alongside him, Keith brought the phone call to an end. "Right, Joe, the cops are on their way. I've told 'em I have seventy passengers plus luggage for the Monarch Hotel, and they're getting onto Blackpool transport for a double-decker bus. They'll send a van out to collect the baggage. For now, we should get everyone off and I need to check the bus over for damage."

He pulled the lever to open the bus door, and a second one to raise the luggage panels. Keith was first off the bus and while he began a walk-round inspection, Joe climbed off and waited at the door for his club members to alight, guiding them beyond the hard shoulder and onto the fresh grass of the verges.

Further up the slip road, three other vehicles, two cars and a light van, were also on the hard shoulder, their occupants climbing out to examine whatever damage had been done. Other drivers, using the exit lane, slowed down to see what was going on, and a considerable queue had already begun to back up onto the motorway while drivers took in the scene.

"I do hope we're not going to be too long," Sylvia Goodson said as Joe and Les Tanner helped her from the bus.

"It'll take as long as it takes, Sylvia." Joe looked up into the cloudless, spring sky and took a deep breath of the fresh air. "Besides, it's a beautiful day. Find yourself a little spot on the grass and enjoy the sunshine."

"Excuse me."

Joe turned to find a woman in her mid-forties standing anxiously alongside him.

"What's up, luv?"

"Are you in charge here?"

"Well, sort of. I'm Joe Murray, the organiser for this lot." He jerked his head in the direction of the club members, now spreading themselves on the grass verge.

"I'm Paula Guy. That truck hit our car." She tutted. "Wouldn't you know it? First time I've been to Blackpool since I was a child, I've got the kids in the car with me, and this has to happen. I don't know if I'm supposed to carry on to our hotel."

"The cops are on their way, Paula, so if I were you, I'd just sit tight until they get here. Did it do much damage?"

"I don't think so. It clipped the front wing and knocked us onto the hard shoulder. But the wheel might be buckled or something. You never know, do you?"

"Where are you staying?" Joe asked.

"The Great Northern."

"That's on the front, isn't it? Not far from the tower?"

21

Paula nodded.

"You and how many children?"

"Three."

"Well, I'll tell you what, the police are organising a local bus to pick us up and take us into Blackpool, and we're staying not far from you. If the police won't let you drive your car, I'm sure we can find room for you on it."

Paula's face brightened. "Oh, that's good of you."

"No problem. But stick around. The cops will need a statement from you if only so you can claim on that trucker's insurance."

A much happier woman, Paula hurried back to her car and Joe ambled away from the bus to join his members on the grassy bank, where he found a spot close to Sheila and Brenda, and sat down.

"Awkward, breaking down like this," Brenda said, "but still better than being cooped up in The Lazy Luncheonette."

Joe agreed with a grunt.

It had been a hard winter; heavy snow in January had been followed by high pressure across the north of the country, bringing with it freezing temperatures and icy roads, which had persisted throughout February and early March. Only later in March did the weather finally begin to break. It had dried the grass on the bank, and for Joe, the chance to enjoy the warm, spring air, even if it was at the expense of a road accident, came as a welcome relief from the pressures of work, weather and the excesses of Sanford Borough Council.

Returning from his walk around the bus, Keith would probably have disagreed, but Joe never got the chance to offer the opinion.

"Not just the mirror." Plonking himself on the grass beside Joe, the driver pointed towards the rear of the bus. "Back wheel arch is buckled, too. That's a new panel. The old man'll go through the roof when he gets to know."

"You haven't told him yet?"

22

"I'll see what the filth have to say." Keith checked his watch. "If they ever get here."

***

Kane scanned the four faces of his traffic managers before him. "In summary then, gentleman, and lady," he beamed an apologetic smile on Megan Stafford, "The budget is squeezed. They want us to do more with less. We're going to need to reschedule the runs more efficiently, and take the drivers to their maximum, permissible hours. All right? Right. Let's get to it, then."

Kane's phone rang. Taking it as a cue to leave, his team rose and began to file out. "Dave Kane."

"Mr Kane? Terry Dodd, security on the main gate, sir. Driver Crowther has just turned into the gate. He's clearly drunk and his rig is showing some damage. I'm not sure—"

"WHAT?? What the hell are you talking about, man?"

While the security officer repeated himself, Kane snapped his fingers repeatedly to get Peter Cruikshank's attention.

"Right. Here's what you do. You hold him at the gate. Do not let him get back into that tractor. I'll send a shunter over to move it to Maintenance, and I'll send someone to deal with Crowther. If he really is drunk, we'll need to call the police."

"But his truck is blocking the gates, sir."

"Then get in the rig and move it into the yard."

"I don't have the licence to drive it, Mr Kane."

"Ours is private land, isn't it? You don't need a licence, and it's only like driving your car but bigger. I'll take responsibility. Now get in it, pull it into the yard, then hold Crowther there until I can get someone to move the rig, and the police arrive." Kane cut the connection and spoke to Cruikshank. "Crowther drunk at the main gate, some damage to his rig. Get onto Control, get them to send Alf Sclater to the gate to move the rig, but it goes to the workshops, nowhere else. Call the police.

23

They'll test him here and if he really blathered, they'll take him away. Amy can go to the station with him and then bring him back. Terry Dodd and his pals can hold him at the gate until the cops arrive."

"Gotcha, Dave," Cruikshank replied with obvious gusto. "When I've done that, I'll check the procedures for this situation."

"No." Kane stayed his assistant. "I'll handle this one, Peter. You can stand witness for management." He caught the doubt crossing Cruikshank's features. "I'm not giving Amy Willows an excuse to have a go at you again. You can sit in, but leave it to me. You get Sclater over there and I'll speak to Amy."

***

An hour later, the inner lane of the slip road had been coned off and the area was awash with police cars. Two constables urged passing motorists to move past the scene quickly and alleviate the queues on both the slip road and the motorway.

After a tour of the damage from Keith, Constable Paul Higson stood with Joe and the driver by the coach door, while one of his colleagues guided a local double-decker bus down the slip road in reverse.

"Neither of us got the number," Joe said, when Higson asked, "but I did get the name of the trucking company. Or part of it, at least."

"Go on," the constable invited.

"Tyne Distribution, all spelled in lower case. Must be from up Newcastle way, I reckon."

Higson's bearded face fell visibly. "You're sure about that? It couldn't have been *Ballantyne* Distribution?"

Joe shrugged. "Coulda been. One of the panels did look as if it had been replaced and 'Tyne' might have had something in front of it."

The policeman tutted. "Just what we need." Heaving a sigh,

he went on, "It's good news for you, Mr Lowry, and you and your party, Mr Murray, but bad news for us."

"Why? Is this company above the law?"

"Course not. But they are the single most important employer in the area and they have a lot of influence. Hang on, I'll just get my buddy to call them." Turning away, Higson called to his colleague further up the slip road, taking a statement from Paula Guy. "Alan: word is the rogue truck was one of Ballantynes. Can you call them, see if they know anything?"

"Will do."

Higson turned to Joe and Keith again. "Shan't be a minute."

"How did you mean it's good from our point of view?" Joe demanded.

The constable nodded to each as he addressed them. "If their driver has created any problems for you and your party, Mr Murray, Ballantynes will compensate. It'll be Ballantynes' wrecker which tows your bus away, Mr Lowry, and they'll take it to their maintenance shed, where they'll repair it. It'll be like new by Monday morning."

Keith shook his head. "I can't authorise that. I'll need to speak to my boss."

"Rest assured, they'll do that, and they'll persuade him. That's Ballantynes, you see. Won't have their name besmirched under any circumstances. You'll have to go to their place, and write out a statement, and you'll need a reliable witness, but they'll take care of everything from there." He smiled wanly. "But from our point of view, they tend to cut us out of the loop until they've carried out an internal investigation. We have hell's teeth of a job getting anything out of them."

"Hang on, hang on," Joe complained. "The way that driver came along this slip road and rammed us and those cars off the road, it's like he was drunk. If so, he could end up in prison. It's not just a motoring offence, is it? It's criminal."

"Yes, we know that, Mr Murray, and they won't obstruct

legal proceedings, but they make it difficult for us to get started. That's all I'm saying." Higson chewed his lip. "It would be very unusual for one of Ballantynes to be under influence. I'm not saying it doesn't happen, but they're really strict over it."

Constable Alan Trench ambled towards them and addressed Higson. "Just been onto Ballantynes, Paul, and they've got him. Coupla lads on their way out to breathalyse him and take a statement, but Ballantynes are insistent it has to be done on their premises because they want to get their internal procedures moving."

Higson shrugged at Joe and Keith. "See what I mean."

"This all sounds a bit iffy to me," Joe grumbled.

"It'll all pan out, Mr Murray. If the driver tests positive, he'll be arrested and interviewed at the station before being sent back to Ballantynes. Now why don't you get your people onto the replacement bus, and we'll get the van drivers started on transferring your luggage."

Chapter Three

"How's the room, Keith?" Joe asked.

With the time coming up to two in the afternoon, he and the bus driver were in a taxi heading along the promenade to Ballantyne Distribution's site, near Squires Gate Airport.

It was Good Friday and the seafront was thick with visitors, the multiple lanes of the dual carriageway were packed with cars travelling in both directions, crowded trams making their way north and south along the tracks, the sun beaming down from a cloudless sky, and Joe wished he had not volunteered to witness the accident report. He would have preferred to be taking the sun and sea air.

"Not bad, Joe," said Keith, answering Joe's question. "I'm up on the top floor with the other nonentities, like the staff, but to be fair it was all they could arrange at such short notice. I'm sharing with a dining room waiter."

"Sounds as bad as mine," Joe grumbled.

The Monarch Hotel stood to one side of the seaward end of Talbot Square. A dour, art deco building constructed of white stone which had long since weathered to a dull grey. Allocated a first floor room, he discovered that his window faced north and while the room was comfortable enough, he knew he would see nothing of the sun.

The view was lively, but uninspiring. On the other side of the square stood the redbrick-built Exchequer pub and restaurant, and to his left, on the seafront was the stark obelisk of the war memorial and just beyond it, the North Pier. He could sit in the widow and watch the cars and buses run up and down the square, he could glance to his left and watch the people, traffic and trams on the promenade but there was nothing of the traditional sights that made Blackpool the town that it was: The Tower, the Pleasure Beach, the sky-scraping arch of The Big One. They were all south of this location.

"We're not much better off," Brenda had complained when they met in the bar an hour after checking in. "Our window overlooks the seafront, and all we can see is the sea."

"And the Central Pier, and the Pleasure Beach," Sheila added.

"If you lean over a bit," Brenda smiled.

The bar, all potted palms and dark wood panelling, was dimly lit, too. Flickering wall lights added a gas or candlelit ambience to the room, which was belied by the modern music whispering softly from wall-mounted speakers, the range of modern pumps on the bar, and the twitter of electronic cash registers as smartly attired bar staff rang up sales.

With typical speed, the Sanford 3rd Age Club had all but commandeered the place. Les and Sylvia sat with Alec and Julia Staines under one of the windows, and across the room, George Robson and Owen Frickley were setting up a game of pool, while Mort Norris and his wife were engaged in what looked like an argumentative debate with Cyril Peck and Mavis Barker.

"Probably reminiscing on how Blackpool was in the fifties when they first came here," Joe commented as he and his two companions descended on an empty table in the centre of the room.

Brenda put on a broad, caricatured, northern accent. "You could have a good night out, a bag of chips, get your legover and still have change from a pound."

"Yeah, well these days, you can't even get the bag of chips for a pound never mind your legover." Joe sipped at a glass of beer and grimaced. "And the beer ain't what it used to be, either."

The two women had gone off for an afternoon of shopping, while Joe waited at the Monarch for Keith to make arrangements, after which they climbed into the taxi for the journey to Ballantyne Distribution.

"I should have been home tonight," Keith grumbled. "It's all right the old man saying I have to stay here, but the missus will be going up the wall. We're supposed to be going to her sister's in Leeds over the weekend."

"I'm sure she'll get over it. And think of the overtime."

"What overtime? You don't think the gaffer's paying me, do you? I get my overnight allowance and that's all. I don't go back on pay until Monday, when I take you lot home … assuming the bus is repaired by then."

"Your boss sorted it with Ballantynes, did he?" Joe asked as their taxi sped past the heaving crowds at the Pleasure Beach.

"They rang him apparently. They'll do all the repair work at their expense, and it'll be shipshape and Bristol fashion by first thing Monday. They'll also reimburse our taxi fares and there'll be some kind of payment for the inconvenience, but I bet I won't see any of that."

"I bet the 3rd Age Club won't, either," Joe said.

Five minutes later, the taxi dropped them at the gates of Ballantyne Distribution's premises opposite the airport. As they climbed out, Joe watched a passenger jet hurtle along the runway and into the air over the sea, and for a moment, he was transported back to the previous September when he, Sheila and Brenda had flown off to Malaga and the Costa del Sol. An excellent, hot and sunny break, which had finally seen him kick the smoking habit, and helped invigorate him for the coming winter.

They approached the gatehouse where a security officer was dealing with an outbound lorry, and while Joe and Keith waited, Joe looked beyond the tall railing fences at the vast buildings inside.

It was a huge complex of buildings, covering at least a couple of acres. In common with most people, he was familiar with Ballantyne Mail Order. He had one of their catalogues somewhere at home. His view of the site reminded him that even in this day and age of economic gloom, low spending and high unemployment, Ballantyne remained one of the most profitable retail outfits in the country.

To one end he could see lines of semi-trailers waiting, he assumed, for loading, unloading or driving away to another, smaller, distribution depot. Closer to the gate were staff car parks, and just beyond them, lines of tractor units ready to hitch up to those trailers. As he watched, tugs, similar to those working on containerbases at docks all over the world, towed trailers to and from the loading bays, to and from the parking lines.

Joe guessed it would be an incredibly complex operation and as always, such mammoth efforts made him wonder how they actually came together. Running The Lazy Luncheonette was complicated enough, so how these people coped, he could not imagine.

"Help you?"

The question brought Joe back from his mental meanderings. It came from the tall, square-shouldered security officer, his name tag identifying him as T. Dodd. The peak of his cap, gleaming in the afternoon sun, was bent almost flat to his forehead, practically touching his hooked nose. At the waist, a large bunch of keys rattled on one side, while on the other, a long, heavy duty flashlight swayed as he walked. He held his clipboard and pen at the ready, his belly bulged towards them, and his pug face was compressed into a scowl of authority, like an overweight police officer suspecting criminal intent. Ex-military or ex-prison service, Joe decided.

"Joe Murray and Keith Lowry from Sanford. One of your trucks hit our bus this morning and we were told to come here, make a statement and your people will put the bus right."

Dodd breathed out heavily, the sigh spelling out his exasperation. "Another one." He scribbled something on his clipboard using his pen as a pointer, he indicated the giant building two hundred yards away, directly ahead of them.

"That's the Sort Centre. You'll find the main entrance on that side." He pointed to the right. "Go in there, report to security. They'll sign you in and take you through to Dispatch, and once you sign in, you're liable for search." The guard now pointed down to yellow parallel lines on the ground. Three feet apart, they were marked with pedestrian icons. "Stick to the marked footpaths and watch out for lorries and shunters."

"Shunters?" Joe asked. "You have a railway line in there?"

The guard scowled further and pointed to one of the yellow tugs towing a trailer at speed around the yard. "The guys driving the tugs are called shunters."

"And what do they call people like you? Warders or just plain screws?"

"Now look—"

"Keep your tights on, pal. Liable for a search." Joe dropped his sneering tone. "Come on, Keith."

As they wandered along the marked footpath, following it towards the building, then off to the right, the car park reminded Joe of a visit he had made to a car factory on the outskirts of Liverpool. There were simply hundreds and hundreds of cars, even if these were mostly second hand, and no empty spaces.

From this point, no more than thirty yards from the building, it was still a long walk to the entrance. They moved to the right, then along the end, where they crossed the roadway used by the shunters and lorry drivers.

A tug pulled up to let them cross. As they reached the pathway alongside the main sort building, the driver slid open his window.

"Where's your hi-vis vest?" he shouted.

"Under me low-vis shirt," Joe called back. "What the hell are you on about?"

The shunter fingered his day-glow yellow vest. "High visibility clothing. It's compulsory. You can't walk round this yard without one."

"We just did," Joe replied.

The shunter reached for his radio. "I'll have to report it. Health and Safety will have you for it."

"Yes, well, tell Health and Safety that if they want me, I don't come cheap."

While the shunter remonstrated, Joe turned his back and he and Keith walked on.

"He's right, you know, Joe. It's all health and safety these days."

"I know. I do employ three people. But right now, I'm supposed to be having a weekend off, and I'm not best pleased at you dragging me into your accident claims."

"No problem. The next time a wagon's gonna hit me, I'll ask him to make sure you're not on the bus."

The size of the building was not truly apparent from the gatehouse. It was only as they made the entrance, that Joe became truly aware of it. If, as he suspected, it was square, then it was a good 100 metres on a side and had a floor area of 10,000 square metres. And, looking at it, it was not all on one level. There were small windows in at least two upper floors. Climbing the few steps to the works entrance, Joe found even the thought of the place mind-numbing.

Leading the way in through the glass doors, he found himself confronted with a small security station of Formica fascias and fake, potted plants. There was a small occasional table surrounded by chairs, and behind the counter were two uniformed officers, one male the other female, monitoring CCTV images on a four-way, split screen. To one side was a narrow entrance which led into the building, surrounded by a scanner, the kind in use at airports, and alongside it was a pair of double doors.

The middle-aged man, his badge identifying him as Reg Barnes, stood up and crossed to his counter.

Joe announced them. "Joe Murray and Keith Lowry. We're here to make a report on an accident with one of your vehicles."

Reg, short but no less rotund than Mr Dodd on the gate, looked him up and down. "So you're the ones without hi-vis vests?"

"Not you, too?" Joe tutted. "I can't speak for Keith, but I am wearing a vest. It's under my shirt and it's plain white, not hi-vis. I need it to keep the chill of my chest. Right? Now can you get someone here to see us?"

The guard took out his pen and opened up a large, hardbound notebook. "Everyone on this site has to wear a hi-vis vest. It's a breach of health and safety regulations to be without one. I'll have to log it in my book."

Joe glanced at his watch. "Now listen to me, sport, I'm here for a weekend break. I've already had some little Hitler on the main gate giving me earache about searches, and I've had a barney with one of your tug drivers, so I'm not really in a mood for your nitpicking."

"But it's a breach of regulations to be without a hi-vis vest," Reg repeated, "and I have to report it."

"I don't care if it's a breach of the peace or a breach of the nuclear proliferation treaty or breach of your britches. Get someone out to see us."

"I have to make a note of this." The guard insisted. Pen poised, he leaned on his counter. "Name?"

"I already told you my name. Joe Murray and he's Keith Lowry."

"Department?" asked the guard.

"What?"

"What department do you work in?"

"We don't work in any department," Joe said. "Or are you considering hiring me just so you can fill in your forms?"

Poring over his incident book, Reg scratched his head. "It says here, I have to log your department, but if you don't work here, how can I?"

"You're saying this as though you think I should give a toss," Joe said.

33

The guard turned away from Joe. "Sandra, this book's all wrong. It's only for employees. Don't we have one for visitors?"

Sandra, who between periods of watching the CCTV, had her nose buried in a magazine on hair care, shrugged. "It's there somewhere." She did not stop reading to reply.

Using his pen, the guard dug out a chunk of earwax and aimed it at the waste bin. "I don't know what I'm supposed to about this."

"See your doctor. He'll syringe your ears."

Reg's features coloured again and the argument could have exploded there and then but for the arrival of a short and stout, middle-aged man, who came in from the yard.

"Something wrong, Reg?" he asked.

"These, er, gentlemen are on site without proper safety clothing, Mr Kane."

Joe noticed immediately that the portly newcomer was wearing a lemon coloured, day-glow jacket over his white shirt. It looked too warm and uncomfortable for the weather, and as if to reinforce that opinion, sweat rolled from his chubby forehead. To make matters worse, when he moved, the jacket swayed as if the pockets were lined with heavy weights.

"If we're supposed to have this gear, why didn't the security man at the main gate issue it?" Joe demanded.

The newcomer flashed a reassuring smile at Reg. "I'll deal with it." Turning to Joe, he asked, "May I ask, who are you and what you want?"

His patience wearing thin, Joe said for the third time, "I'm Joe Murray and this is Keith Lowry. One of your drivers hit our bus on the motorway this morning and we were asked to come here and provide a statement. Keith is the bus driver and I'm his witness."

"Ah. I'm Dave Kane, the Transport Manager." He offered a sweating hand and Joe shook it. "I've just been over to our workshop to, er… to assess the damage to our truck, your bus and the other vehicles." Kane checked his watch. "I'm sorry for the trouble we've put you to, Mr Murray, and I'll have to delay you a short while longer. Could I ask you to wait here for about another ten minutes? I need to get to the dispatch office, change out of this damn thing," He fingered the high visibility jacket, "and pick up the necessary report forms. I'll have one of the staff in the Sort Centre bring you out a cup of coffee." He smiled encouragingly. "And you're right by the way. The security man on the gate should have issued you with a hi-vis vest." He marched through the double doors into the building.

Barely mollified, Joe and Keith sat down, and soon a member of staff came from the interior and left coffee with them. A while later, Terry Dodd, the security officer who had greeted them on the gate, arrived, and promptly got into an argument with Reg.

"You should have issued these people with hi-vis clothing, Terry."

"Don't you think I have enough to do on the gate? I'm on my own, I've incoming and outgoing traffic to deal with, and you expect me to issue protective clothing to every muppet who walks through the gate. *You* give 'em the hi-vis vests." Having delivered his abrupt opinion, Dodd marched through the scanner, causing it to bleep, and into the building.

Reg shook his head. "Bad tempered sod, that one."

Joe assumed Reg was talking to his colleague, but he took the opportunity to comment. "I'm not so sure he should be calling us muppets, either."

It would be almost twenty minutes before Kane reappeared wearing a dark blue blazer, carrying a set of forms, and full of apologies. "I had to go up to my office and it's on the third floor," he explained. Setting the forms on the table, he took out his pen. "Now, gentlemen, all I need from you is an account of what happened. We've spoken to your boss, Mr Lowry—"

"Yeah," Keith interrupted. "He told me."

"Ah. Good. You'll know, then, that we've guaranteed to have your vehicle repaired and roadworthy again by Monday morning. You'll be able to pick it up first thing. We'll also reimburse any out of pocket expenses for yourself, including taxi fares."

"What happened to the driver?" Joe demanded.

"I think that's our concern."

"Sure. But I was just thinking, it's a neat way of you avoiding the law, isn't it? Hauling the driver in here and coming to your own conclusions."

Kane sighed. "We don't avoid the law, Mr Murray. When the driver returned, we held him here until the police arrived. They breathalysed him, found him over the limit and they've charged him. Once that was done, we put our disciplinary procedures in place." Kane allowed a moment's silence, then went on. "Ballantyne Distribution is conscious of its public image. It's true, we don't like our name in the headlines, especially in a negative sense, but we do not condone any of our employees breaking the law, and we will come down hard on this man."

He began to fill in the headings on the form.

Joe was about to comment on corporate control of the media, but before he could say anything, three more security guards rushed through the scanner and made for the exit.

With the scanner bleeping loudly at the intrusion, Reg leapt from his seat.

"Panic on, Reg," one of the guards explained. "Those idiots in Maintenance are chariot racing with the wheelie bins again. Terry Dodd and two others have gone out through the Dispatch exit."

"Nobody told me," Reg said with great indignation.

"Only just come through."

Kane paused in completing his forms. "Hey," he barked. "When you get over there, I want names. D'you understand? Don't just break it up. Get me names."

"Yes, Mr Kane."

The Transport Manager turned back to Joe and Keith. "Sorry about that. We have a bunch of apprentices in the workshop and they get out of hand. It's like dealing with schoolboys."

"And are these the same kids who are working on my bus?" Keith asked, his forehead lined with worry.

Kane replied with a wan smile. "Let's get these forms filled in, eh?"

Calm had descended on the reception area once more. Kane began to go through the details of the accident with Joe and Keith, Sandra continued studying her magazine, and Reg took his seat alongside her, his gaze switching between the wall clock and the CCTV screens. The minutes ticked by, Reg yawned consistently, Kane asked questions, Joe and Keith answered as best they could, and with the time just after three o'clock, Kane finally passed the form to the two men for their signatures.

And at that moment, Peter Cruikshank staggered through the scanner, one hand clutched to the back of his neck.

The scanner beeped loudly, stirring Reg, attracting the attention of the three men at the coffee table. Joe looked up in time to see Cruikshank's eyes roll up into their sockets, just before he folded and crumpled to the composition floor.

Joe was first to the prone man, kneeling over him, first listening to his breathing and then gingerly pressing a finger to his neck.

Joe stood again. "He's alive. Only just. Dial nine, nine, nine and get an ambulance."

"We need a first-aider," Reg insisted.

"Never mind your first-aider. He needs paramedics." Joe stood up and fished for his mobile phone as Reg protested further.

"There are procedures, Mr Murray, he needs to be looked at by a first-aider who'll then—"

Ignoring him, Joe tossed his mobile to Keith. "Call an ambulance." Swinging his attention to Reg, he said, "You, bell the main gate, tell them to let the medic in and direct them to this door."

His face flustered, Reg, nevertheless picked up the phone and

Joe concentrated on Kane. "What's his name?"

"Cruikshank. Peter Cruikshank."

Joe nodded and after studying a livid weal on the back of Cruikshank's neck, gently rolled the man over.

"Peter," he said loudly. "Can you hear me, Peter? I'm Joe. You've been hurt, but you need to stay with me, Peter."

Keith passed the phone to Joe. "They want to talk to someone who knows what's what."

Joe took it from him and spoke urgently into it. "We need paramedics, double quick. Ballantyne Distribution, the main entrance to the building. Man looks like he's been struck on the back of the neck or fallen against something... No, no, he's alive, but he's not moving, his breathing is shallow and he has a nasty weal on the back of his neck. It may be broken... Right... Right... My name? Joe Murray... Okay." He snapped off the phone and put it back in his pocket. "Paramedics are on the way. They say, don't move him. Let them handle it."

Facing him, Reg fumed. "You had no authority to make that call."

"What?"

Reg jabbed an irritated finger into the air ahead of Joe's chest. "There are procedures. All accidents must be attended by a suitably qualified first-aider, and only he has the authority to call—"

Joe snatched the finger, held onto it and glowered. "Have you ever seen anyone die?"

"Well, er, no, but—"

"Have you ever seen anyone who has just died in terrible pain?"

"Well, er, no, but—"

"Well until you have, don't rattle on to me about what I'm authorised and not authorised to do. When you have someone this badly injured, every second counts. Now that the professionals are on their way, you can call your first-aider and let him fill in his stupid, bloody forms." Joe turned back and crouched over the injured man again. "Peter. Can you hear me, Peter? Don't try to move or anything. We've got help coming."

A young man stepped through the scanner, setting it off once more. He carried a booklet of official looking forms in one hand, and a first aid kit in the other. He spoke briefly to Reg and Kane, and then concentrated on Joe.

"I'm Wayne Allthorpe. I understand you called the ambulance, Mr Murray? Are you qualified in first aid?"

"No, but I'm qualified as a human being, and it was obvious that this man couldn't be moved and needed urgent medical attention. Not first aid; medical."

"Yes, but we have systems in place, and you can't simply shortcut them. The company won't accept responsibility unless an authorised person has dealt with the matter. You don't even work here."

"The way you people prat about, I'm glad," Joe retorted.

"Yes, but…"

Wayne trailed off at a wheezing gasp from Cruikshank. Both he and Joe bent to the injured man.

Wayne pressed an ear to Cruikshank's chest. "No heartbeat."

Joe pressed Cruikshank's eyelids back. "Pupils are dilating. He's probably arrested. You got a face mask?"

Wayne snapped open the first aid kit and retrieved the mask. Slipping it over his head and across his face, he said to Joe. "Two and thirty. I'll breathe, you compress."

"Go."

Joe found it hard work. Wayne would breathe twice into Cruikshank's mouth, applying pressure to the central chest area to expel the breath, then Joe would go with thirty chest compressions in fifteen seconds. After only a minute, sweat began to pour from Joe's forehead.

Others stood by, watching in awe while the first-aider and the stranger worked to keep the dying man alive. By the time the paramedics arrived, Joe was all but exhausted.

While one connected them by phone to the nearest hospital,

the other broke out their equipment and took over from Joe and Wayne. When the second paramedic had the hands-free connection set up, he joined his colleague and they began to work on Cruikshank.

Joe backed off, sat down, and mopped the sweat from his brow.

"You're pretty cool, Joe," Keith said to him.

"Then how come I'm sweating?"

"No. I meant cool, as in calm. Y'know. In an emergency."

"Do you know how many emergencies I've had down the years?" Joe watched the paramedics set up the ECG and soon afterwards, the defibrillation equipment. "Ovens catching fire, boiling fat spilled on bare arms? Slips and falls on kitchen floors? You learn, mate, to keep your head."

"Mr Lowry is right," Kane said. "If Peter comes through this, it'll be you he has to thank."

Joe stared grimly at Cruikshank as the body jerked slightly under the electric jolt of a defibrillator. "If he survives, it'll be God he needs to thank."

"I thought dead people jumped out of the skin when they did this to them," Keith said, leaving Joe to wade through the impersonal pronouns in an effort to work out who was doing what to whom.

Wayne obviously had a better grasp of the driver's generalisations. "That's drama. It's done for effect. In reality, there is some muscle contraction during defibrillation, but not much."

Silence fell over the security station while the paramedics worked on Cruikshank, but as time progressed Joe knew that they were fighting a battle already lost. After a further ten minutes, one stood and faced them, his features grim. Joe had seen that look before: on the night his father died, on the day his mother passed away.

"I'm sorry. He's gone."

Behind the counter, Sandra, her magazine forgotten, burst

into tears and Reg comforted her.

Having been expecting it, Joe took out his phone, positioned himself behind Cruikshank's head, crouched and examined the injury.

He had obviously been struck with some force. The impact had left an angry weal, displaying the cross-hatched pattern Joe had mentioned, and he suspected that the point of maximum impact was where it was at its most livid, dead centre of the wound, just under the base of Cruikshank's skull.

Lining up his phone, he took two photographs.

"Might I ask what you're doing?" Kane demanded.

"Gathering evidence before all these trampling feet and wannabe helpers disturb it."

"You're a police officer, are you?"

"Nope, but you're going to need them."

Kane clucked impatiently. "What I need is to contact the Health and Safety Executive."

Joe disagreed instantly. "Call the police."

He said it with such conviction that all eyes turned on him.

"This wasn't an accident. It was murder."

Chapter Four

"I love the taste of Campari at the seaside." Brenda put down her glass and beamed a broad smile on Sheila. "Face facts, we have it pretty cushy, don't we?"

Surrounded by carrier bags bearing famous, High Street names, the two women had enjoyed several hours of shopping and were seated in the bar of The Exchequer, on the far side of Talbot Square from their hotel. The pub was busy, but not overcrowded, and both were glad to be off their feet.

More delicately than her best friend, Sheila sipped at her port and lemon. "I think we deserve it, Brenda. Haven't we worked all our lives to have it cushy at our age? It's just a shame it couldn't have been like this a few years back. When we were both young enough to enjoy it."

"What's age got to do with it? I'm still young enough to service a toyboy's requirements." Brenda laughed. "But he'd have to be a wealthy one. Like him, there."

Sheila followed Brenda's eye to a tall, dark-haired man at the far end of the bar. In his late thirties, he was casually, but expensively dressed in light grey slacks and a crisp, short-sleeved shirt which showed off his fine biceps. On his left wrist was a Rolex, or similarly high-priced watch. He held a half empty glass of lager in one hand and as he drank from it, he noticed Brenda looking and smiled at her.

She smiled back. "Hey up, I think I might have trapped off here," she said to Sheila.

"Brenda, you are completely incorrigible."

"If it's fun, go for it, I always say."

He detached himself from the bar and wove his way through

the tables and stood before them. "It's Mrs Riley and Mrs Jump, isn't it?"

Brenda's jaw dropped. Her look of astonishment, mingled with disappointment, caused Sheila to laugh.

"Forgive me," Sheila said to the stranger. "Neither my friend nor I were aware that you knew us."

"I know of you, ladies," he said, "but we've never met." He gripped the back of the chair opposite Brenda. "May I join you?"

Brenda could only nod.

He sat down and placed his half of lager on the table. "My name is Gerard Vaughan. I know your friend and employer, Joe Murray." He looked around as if seeking Joe. "He's not with you?"

At last recovering her composure, Brenda cleared her throat. "No. He, er, he had business to deal with."

A rueful smile played about his lips. "Business? On Easter weekend? Here in Blackpool?"

"That's Joe," Sheila said. "A driven man."

"Driven by the profit motive," Brenda agreed. "As you must know if you know him."

"Indeed." Vaughan played with his glass, his dark eyes fixed on it as he moved it on the coaster. It seemed important to him to ensure it sat dead centre of the brewery logo covering the beer mat. "I was hoping to catch him. Invite him to dinner this evening." He looked up and smiled again at them. "I'm staying at the Hilton, and Joe and I have some business matters to discuss. Perhaps you two ladies would pass the message on and naturally, you would be more than welcome to join us."

"The Hilton?" Brenda had an instant and pleasing vision of dinner with Vaughan … alone in the sumptuous surroundings of the renowned hotel chain. "We'd be delighted."

"I'm sure Joe would, too," Sheila said, "but forgive me, Mr Vaughan, why haven't you rung Joe? He has his mobile with him."

"I think he would turn me down, Mrs Riley. He's such an independent man, isn't he? Likes to pay his way. I thought if I could catch him with you, he might be a little more amenable."

Brenda laughed. "I've heard Joe Murray called a lot of things, but amenable isn't one of them."

Vaughan stood. "I'd be grateful if you could pass the invitation on. Shall we say seven thirty for eight?" With a nod, he took his leave of them.

Brenda smacked her lips. "Can you distract Joe while I work on Mr Vaughan?"

She was surprised to find Sheila not smiling, but looking concerned. "I think there is something very fishy about that man, and I would be very surprised if Joe actually knows him."

"Well he knew all about Joe … and us."

"That's not the same as Joe knowing about him, dear."

***

Across town, faced with a babble of protest at his announcement, Joe rode it out, allowing it to wind down naturally before holding up his hands for complete silence.

"All right, all right. Murder might be a bit strong. What I'm really saying is, this man did not die by accident. Trust me on this. I've investigated enough murders to spot the signs."

The senior paramedic challenged him. "You're an expert, are you? Medically trained?"

"Nope. I'm not even a cop. Just a private detective… of sorts… with a reputation for spotting everything." He strode over to Cruikshank's inert form, bent and rolled the body over. "Look at that bruising," he said, pointing to the neck.

Both paramedics examined the wound, which showed a livid red, encircled with blue, its surface marked with a cross-hatched pattern.

"Lot of internal bleeding," said the senior man, "possibly bone and nerve damage. One hell of a blow, for sure." He stood

44

up straight. "But he might have slipped, fallen and hit his neck on something."

"Like what? Look properly at the injury," Joe said. "If he slipped and fell, the wound would have been to the back of his head. It isn't. It's on his neck. And how do you explain that unusual pattern?"

The paramedic pondered for a moment. "He could have slipped on a staircase and hit his head against one of the risers as he was going up … or more likely, down. And maybe the staircase has that kind of pattern on the flat."

"Whether he was going up or down, he would have rolled further, so where are the rest of his bruises? He'd have knocked his face, his hands, and so on. You see any other marks on him?" Joe took in all his audience. "This man was struck on the back of the neck by a heavy implement, and he died as a result of that injury. I'll stake my reputation on it, and you, Mr Kane, need to call the cops, not Health and Safety."

"And I say you're being too hasty," the paramedic argued. "Only a pathologist can confirm what you're saying, and as long as he was fit, healthy and there's no medical reason to account for his death, there will be a post mortem."

His features bright red, sweat bathing his forehead, Kane cut in on the argument. "All right, all right. That's enough." Digging into his pocket, he pulled out a handkerchief and as he did so, Joe noticed a black cord, formed into a loop like a wrist strap, left dangling. Kane hurriedly tucked it back into the pocket and mopped the sweat from his brow. "Mr, Murray, I'm grateful for your input on this, but like our friend here said, there is nothing to point to any third party involvement. I need to ring the police, certainly, but it's a matter of routine. If any other evidence should turn up or if the Health and Safety people are suspicious, they will inform the police. But right now, it looks like a tragic accident." He nodded to Reg. "Ring both, please."

While Reg moved back from the counter to carry out the

task, Joe shrugged. "Have it your own way. But will the HSE know what they're looking at? They'll assume, just like you, that he fell down the stairs or something. I'm saying he didn't. He has been struck on the back of the neck."

Kane looked again to the paramedic, who mirrored Joe's shrug. "My job is to save lives where I can, not to work out how someone might have hit the back of his head."

"Or got hit." Addressing Kane, Joe asked, "Where does Peter work?"

Kane appeared distracted, and it was as if Joe's question brought him back to the here and now. "Hmm? What? Oh, sorry. He was my deputy. Divided his time between our office on the third floor and the dispatch office on this level." Kane waved vaguely through the scanner. "Other end of the building from here."

"But you don't know where he was before he turned up here?"

"Well, I know where he was a little while ago. Third floor. He was there when I called in to change my jacket."

"And he was okay?"

Kane nodded.

"Would he come down by lift?" Joe demanded.

Kane promptly shook his head. "I know Peter. He kept himself fit, and he never used the lift. Besides, our lifts are not just for personnel. They're for goods, too, and they tend to be slow. He could be up the stairs before the lift, never mind down."

Joe slotted the information into his agile mind, and put it into some kind of order.

"Okay. We know he was fine at, say, ten to three. He needed to come downstairs for something, but we don't know what, unless he told someone else up there. We assume he used the stairs, so does the staircase have any kind of non-slip plates which would cause that curious kind of bruising?"

Kane sighed. "I don't know, Mr Murray. I've been using the

stairs and the lift for years, and quite frankly, I just haven't taken that much notice."

"That's the trouble with this world," Joe complained. "No one notices anything."

Reg returned from the rear of his station to lean on the counter with that self-satisfied air of one who has done his job. "Police and Health and Safety on their way, Mr Kane."

"Thank you, Reg."

While one paramedic began to pack away their equipment the other set about writing the report. Wayne also began to fill in his forms. Kane looked round the small group and shrugged, almost as if he were embarrassed.

"Well, I don't think there's anything else we can do, other than wait for the authorities to arrive. I'd like to thank you for your efforts, Mr Murray."

"No problem. If the police need to speak to me, I'm staying at the Monarch."

"Right. The Monarch. Well, thanks again."

"There is just one thing," Keith said. "My bus. The claim form."

"Oh. Of course. You want a copy of it, don't you?" Kane fussed at the coffee table, sorting out the documents they had completed. When he had them in satisfactory order, he passed them to Reg. "Copy those for me, please." While waiting for the copies, he spoke again to Keith. "You have my personal assurance that the bus will be ready first thing Monday morning. If you present your employer with receipts for out of pocket expenses, taxi fares, hotel bills and so on, we'll ensure they're paid, too." Reg handed him the documents, and he passed the warm copies to Keith. "The same goes for you, Mr Murray, and if any of your members feel they have a claim against us, don't hesitate to get in—"

"Dave! Dave! Quick!"

Coming from the entrance, the urgent voice of the shunter Joe had argued with, cut Kane off.

"Alf? What is it?"

Alf's agitated features worked worriedly, his mouth quivering as he replied. "Stan Crowther. He's spark out on park fifteen. I think he's dead."

The paramedics exchanged glances. Kane caught their eye and as if some unspoken agreement had passed between them, the medics hurried out, Kane calling after them, "Follow Alf." The manager turned on Reg. "I'll cut through the Sort Centre. Don't move Peter."

"I'll come with you," Joe said and followed Kane through the scanner.

Joe heard Reg shouting after him. "Hey, you can't go through there." But by then, he had already gone through.

Hurrying to catch up with Kane, Joe found himself in a hive of activity where the noise produced by the rattling of machinery and constant chatter of the workers was deafening.

Above him a complex arrangement of conveyors carried parcels around the vast warehouse and occasionally, a tray tipped up, pouring its contents onto chutes, for them to flow down to the loading bay where warehouse hands loaded them onto trailers. Around the packed floor area were larger items; furniture, bicycles, large toys, keep fit equipment, cages of clothing and pallets of catalogues. Men and women carrying computer printouts, worked quickly, but efficiently to pick and load the items. Here and there were enclosed rest areas, decked with vending machines and rows of tables and chairs which instantly reminded Joe of The Lazy Luncheonette. Judging by the small number of people using them, they were about as busy as The Lazy Luncheonette, too.

Kane hurried along a broad gangway, occasionally dodging an electric truck carrying heavy items, weaving around people as they went about their work, and at the far end, he pushed through a wooden door marked *Dispatch*.

Joe followed and as the door closed behind him the noise from the warehouse was snuffed out. Instead, he found himself in a narrow corridor, male and female toilets to the left, one door at right angles to him, which led into an office, and another directly ahead, leading to the drivers' rest room.

Kane rushed straight through, barely acknowledging the two drivers taking their break. He turned right, through yet another door. Joe followed, shot past a counter where a driver was receiving instructions from one of the staff, and was right on Kane's heels as the manager passed through a metal door, to the outside.

After the soft, interior lighting, the harsh sunlight strained Joe's eyes for a moment. He was in the north yard, the sun high and slightly to his left. From here, he could see Blackpool Tower and the tall arch of The Big One on the Pleasure Beach. But they were the only landmarks he could see. To the left, in the west yard were the monolithic buildings he seen when he first arrived while ahead of him and to his right were rows and rows of semi-trailers in the distinctive green and white livery of Ballantyne Distribution.

The trailers were parked at an angle to the building, so aside from a couple of rows immediately to the left, he could not see down the lines between them. They were three deep and ran all the way back to a wire mesh fence.

He was presented with a short flight of steps. Kane had already hurried down them and turned to his right, making for the trailers where the paramedics and the shunter had parked. Joe hurried in pursuit, noticing that the lanes of trailers were clearly marked out with yellow lines, and that each lane was numbered.

Thinking to himself that for one so obviously overweight, Kane was pretty nimble, he watched the numbers flash past on the ground; 10, 11, 12, 13... Kane turned in between the trailers on parks fifteen and sixteen, and Joe was right on his heels.

At the rear of the second trailer on park fifteen, Alf, the shunter stood agitatedly by, and one of the paramedics was attending the fallen man, while the other listened for information. As Kane and Joe arrived, the first paramedic stood up and shook his head, grimly.

"Sorry, Mr Kane. He's dead."

From the corner of his eye, Joe registered Alf staggering back, and soon it was followed by the sound of him retching.

Silence fell over them, disturbed only by the rumble of a shunter or a lorry passing them, and the crackle of the radio in Alf's cab.

Disregarding it, Joe looked down as the paramedics backed off.

Stan Crowther was half curled into a foetal ball, his right hand stretched out as if he were reaching for something beneath the trailer. The collar of his high visibility jacket was turned up. Careful to avoid cracking his head on the rear of the trailer, Joe bent and peeled the collar back.

"Hey. What the hell are you doing?" the paramedic protested.

"Leave him alone. The police—"

"Need to be called right now," Joe said, and once more dug out his mobile phone.

Crowther had injuries to his neck similar to those Cruikshank had suffered, but this time there appeared to be two, one overlaying the other, at different angles across the back of his neck. The upper injury ran from the left shoulder and crossed the neck just under the base of the skull, the lower one ran straight across the neck, and Joe guessed that the maximum force of impact was where the two injuries crossed, dead centre.

Focussing his phone, he took two pictures from slightly different angles, then backed out from beneath the trailer and straightened up.

He was greeted by a puzzled Dave Kane. "Mr Murray, what are you doing here?"

"Saving your bacon by the looks of it," Joe replied. "Look at him."

"You have no business—" Kane began, only for Joe to cut him off.

"I said look at him. He has the same bruising on the back of his neck as Peter Cruikshank. Some kind of cross-hatch pattern. Only this time, it looks as if he's been hit twice." He pointed down at Crowther's neck. Joe rounded on the paramedics. "So what are you gonna say this time? He hit his head against the steps twice?"

Kane sighed. "Mr Murray, with the best will in the world, you have no business being here. You don't work for Ballantynes and you're not even properly dressed for this yard. Now—"

Joe cut him off again. "What is it with you people and your rules? Right now, Kane, you have not one but two dead men on your site. That is not an accident, and it's not negligence. It's murder and the longer you delay in calling the police, the more you let forensic evidence deteriorate. Now forget my underwear, high-visibility or otherwise, and call the bloody police, man. And I need to be here. They'll want to interview me, too."

Visibly shaken, Kane sighed and looked to the paramedics.

"It does look suspicious," the first admitted. "It could be innocent, but it could be foul play. Whatever, we have to report the matter now, and he's right. You need the cops."

"Reg already called them."

Joe shook his head. "They'll send out uniformed, and you need both CID and Scientific Support."

Kane nodded and dug into his pockets for his mobile phone. Punching in the numbers with a shaking finger, he spoke quickly but lucidly once the connection was made and concluded the call a minute later with an abrupt, "Thanks." Shutting down the phone, dropping it back into his pockets, he said, "The police are on their way. They say we mustn't touch anything or move either of the bodies." He narrowed his irritated stare at Joe. "They'll need to speak to all of us." Now he turned to the paramedics. "Can you stay here with Stan?" On receiving confirmation, he spoke to Joe. "Mr Murray, we can go back inside, and I'll find you some tea or coffee until they get here."

"Sure. Yeah. No problem."

Kane spent a few moments checking that Alf was all right, then led Joe back to the dispatch office.

"Dave," one of the staff called out as they entered. "We've got Reg Barnes at the front door playing hell. He said Peter is in the way and it won't be long before the day shift are signing off. Wants to know if he can move Peter."

Kane looked to Joe for guidance who shook his head. "Didn't you just say the cops told you not to move either of them?"

"I'll sort it," the manager called back as he led Joe to the drivers' rest room. "Get this man a cuppa, will you?" He smiled wanly at Joe. "Sorry about this. Security are a pain in the backside, but for once, they're going to have to let everyone out with passing through the scanner."

"Don't worry about it. Oh, if Keith is still there, tell him to get on his way without me. If I know anything about the cops, this could take a few hours. Hey, and one last thing." He waited for Kane's eyebrows to rise. "Two sugars in my tea."

Chapter Five

Kane left Joe in the drivers' rest room, which was immediately adjacent to the Dispatch office. An ergonomically sound arrangement, in Joe's opinion. If and when called, drivers had only to pass through the far doorway to be at the counter and pick up their orders.

Comprising a dozen tables, each with seating for four, there was the familiar line of vending machines – hot and cold drinks, snacks and confectionery – a water cooler and small sink where users could wash up their cups and plates. Along the wall furthest from the door was a bank of small lockers, four high, ten across. Joe surmised that they would belong to the drivers, but considering the number of such employees a large company like this would have on the books, he guessed many would not have a locker.

Kane left him sharing the rest room with two women from the Dispatch office, one, a petite, thirty-something blonde, making an effort to console the other, a dark haired woman a few years older who was in floods of tears.

"She's heard?" Joe said.

The blonde nodded. "Megan knew both Peter and Stan well." She smiled wanly. "I'm sorry, but I don't know you."

"Joe Murray. I only came here to report the accident with our bus, but I sort of got tangled up in it all."

"I'm Beth Edmunds and this is Megan Stafford. We're both dispatch managers. Do you know what's going on?"

Joe elected for discretion. "Not yet. I'm sure the police will sort it out." He spoke directly to the older woman. "Megan, I don't know if it helps, but neither man suffered much. I don't think they really knew what was happening."

It did not help. Megan was simply reduced to further sobbing.

At length, when her emotions were under better control, the two women returned to their duties and Joe was left alone. Drivers came and went, some going out to the yard to begin their shift, others, having finished for the day, making their way to the Sort Centre and main exit. Now and again, parcel handlers would come in from the Sort Centre and wash out a cup or fill a bottle from the water cooler… and Joe waited.

It was almost five before a uniformed officer finally escorted him through Dispatch to a private office and took his statement. When he had signed it, he was asked to stay where he was until the senior investigating officer gave him clearance to leave, and he waited a further half hour before Chief Inspector Richard Burrows entered the room and with a fierce scowl introduced himself.

"Joe Murray from Sanford. I take you're *the* Joe Murray."

Tall, imposing, in his mid-forties, the chief inspector's brusque manner spoke of a man not to be trifled with, and yet he delivered his words with a directness Joe found refreshing after the inconsequential waffle of the Ballantyne employees.

"There may be other Joe Murrays in Sanford, but I don't know of them," Joe replied. "You've obviously heard of me."

"Oh, yes. Pat Feeney was full of you at the autumn conference last year."

Joe's face lit up with the memory of Chief Inspector Feeney and the days of meandering through the hot summer at Windermere, solving a drug-related murder. "How is Patricia?"

Burrows' features turned even darker. "She was fine the last time I saw her. Ready to jump you if she could ever get near to you again. So impressed with your observational skills." He leaned over Joe. "But I'm not Feeney. I don't' fancy you and I don't need a wannabe Sherlock sticking his nose into cases on my patch. Understand?"

Joe decided it would be easy to cave in to this man. He was well over six feet tall, and powerfully built. He refused, however, to be intimidated. "So what's your conclusion, Burrows? Double murder?"

"My conclusions and my investigation are nothing to do with you, Murray. We have your statement, you can go. Get drunk with your pals, but I don't want to find you anywhere near this place or the case."

"Gonna be bloody awkward when I come with our bus driver to collect our vehicle on Monday, then, isn't it?"

"You know what I mean. Just get out, and don't come back."

"I can see you're one of those who doesn't want the public's co-operation. So—"

"Co-operation is one thing, Murray, but if I catch you shoving your oar in, I'll charge you."

"With what?"

"Try obstructing the police in the course of their inquiries. Now clear off."

Joe sneered. "Obstructing the police, my eye. If my experience is anything to go by, people like you wouldn't notice if someone stole Blackpool Tower."

"Out."

Joe stood up and noticed that even when he was leaning half over the desk, Burrows still towered above him. Affecting a yawn, he said, "Right. Whatever you want. When you come to the wrong conclusion and you need help, I'm staying at the Monarch. Only don't wait too long. We go home on Monday afternoon, and I ain't hanging around longer to work on a murder you people can't crack."

It was Burrows' turn to sneer. "They told me you were a smartarse. For your information, Mr clever dick detective, it's not murder. These two clowns were fighting and it went too far."

Joe hid his surprise. "And they died two hundred yards apart. Must have been one hell of a fight. See ya, Mr clever dick detective."

Joe left the room to be met by Kane.

"Sorry you were kept so long, Mr Murray. I'll escort you through the warehouse to the exit." He turned to a brunette at a nearby desk. "Beth, can you order a taxi for Mr Murray, and put it on our account."

"Thanks," Joe said. "And please call me Joe."

Walking alongside Joe, back through the cacophony of the Sort Centre, Kane raised his voice. "That chief inspector didn't appear too pleased when he heard your name."

"You get used to it," Joe said, raising his voice, too. "Some don't mind accepting help, others, like Burrows, take offence. I'm not gonna worry about it, but you should."

They paused while a warehouse hand picked up a stack of empty pallets on his electric truck and drove them away. While they waited, Joe expanded on his advice.

"Make no mistake, Dave, the cops are very good. In fact when it comes to this kind of thing, they're the best. They have access to services I don't, and those same forensics will get them to the truth and hopefully the killer."

"So what's the problem?" Kane asked.

"Burrows has preconceived ideas. He claims the two men were fighting and killed each other. I don't know where he got this from, but—"

"I do," Kane interrupted as the electric truck moved out of their way. "I'm sorry, Joe, but it's a matter of some confidence. I can't let you in on it."

Falling into step alongside Kane once more, Joe replied, "That's okay. Trouble is, while Burrows is chasing up his theoretical fight between the two men, he may miss the reality of the situation."

"You don't think they were?"

"Let's just say I'd need evidence to back that up. Right now, my guess is there was a third party involved, one man – or woman – who killed them both. Burrows will eventually come

56

to the same conclusion, but in the meantime, it's Easter weekend and he won't press for the post mortem results. That gives the killer, if there is one, time to organise himself and his alibis."

They reached the main exit, where the double doors had been opened. Joe glanced through the scanner as they passed. Peter Cruikshank's body had been removed, but forensic officers in their white overalls, were still busy searching, photographing and dusting for evidence.

Kane vouched for Joe as they made for the door.

Stepping outside, Joe turned to shake hands. "I'm at the Monarch if you need any advice."

"Thanks, Joe, but I think we'll leave it to the police." Kane sighed. "Right now I have to ring the big boss and tell him what's happened. Sir Douglas doesn't like the police on site and he doesn't like anything that could be construed as adverse publicity."

"I know how he feels," Joe replied, "but it'll be tough to keep this out of the papers. See y'around."

***

The evening disco at the Monarch was in full swing. Joe sat with Sheila and Brenda by the windows, looking out on the darkening April sky or watching their fellow members moving around the small dance floor.

Joe had arrived back at the hotel just after six, to be greeted with the news of Vaughan's invitation.

Eager to get to his room, to shower and shave, the news brought Joe up short. "Gerard Vaughan?"

"That's him," Sheila said.

"You don't know who Gerard Vaughan is?"

"We know he's very wealthy," Brenda said. "He must be. He's staying at the Hilton."

"He would. He's the man who's trying to take away your

living."

The two women exchanged cautious glances.

"Gerard Vaughan is the Managing Director of Gleason Holdings," Joe explained. "They and Sanford Borough Council are the ones wanting to knock down The Lazy Luncheonette and put us all out of work."

Sheila's disapproval manifested itself in pursed lips and a frown. Brenda, on the other hand, was fuming. "Wait until I see him again. I'll rip his—"

"Brenda!"

"I was going to say I'll rip his head off."

"Keep away from him," Joe ordered. "He hasn't been able to sway me, so now I figure he's trying to divide and conquer. If you do see him again, threaten to report him for stalking."

And with that, Joe returned to his room.

He had passed much of their evening meal telling his two friends of events at Ballantyne Distribution while they regaled him of their shopping exploits. With the time just after eight, and the sun setting over the Irish Sea, the sound of the Beatles singing *Hey Jude* filling the bar, the day's toil and trouble had begun to take its toll on Joe, who found himself getting sleepier by the minute.

"You need an early night," Sheila told him.

"Alone," Brenda echoed.

"As if I'd be sharing it with anyone. What's the point in going to bed early anyway? I'd only be up in the early hours of the morning."

To his surprise Dave Kane stepped into the room, looked around, spotted him and made his way round the perimeter of the crowded dance floor to join him.

"Hello, Joe. I hope you don't mind me tracking you down like this."

Joe's fatigue left him, instantly supplanted by a feeling of expectation. "Course not, Dave. Let me introduce my two partners in crime; Sheila Riley and Brenda Jump. Ladies, this is

Dave Kane, Transport Manager at Ballantyne Distribution."

Kane secured drinks for them, a Campari and soda for Brenda, port and lemon for Sheila and a half of bitter for Joe, while taking only a glass of lemonade for himself.

"I live outside Blackpool and I have to drive home," he explained.

When they were settled, he leaned across the table to ensure that Joe could hear him over the music.

"After you left, I was on the phone to Sir Douglas Ballantyne, our Chief Executive. He's the majority shareholder, you know, but he doesn't take much of an active role in the business these days. Leaves it all to his son, Toby. Anyway, as I told you, Sir Douglas doesn't like having the law crawling all over the site, and he doesn't like bad publicity. He wants this business cleared up quickly. I told him what you said, and the upshot of it is, Joe, he wants you to investigate."

Unwilling to appear too eager, Joe was about to protest, but Kane carried on.

"He only rang back half an hour ago. In the meantime, he's researched you thoroughly. He knows as much about you as your mother ever did, and he's very impressed with your record. It doesn't matter what you charge, we'll pay, and obviously, we'll cover all your expenses."

The Beatles faded and were replaced by Jeff Beck and *Hi-Ho Silver Lining*. Joe put on pained expression.

"I dunno, Dave. I'm here on a weekend break, you know, and I have other things to worry about."

Kane's chubby brow creased. "Other things to worry about? In Blackpool?"

"No. Back home in Sanford. The local council and a big development company are trying to pull my cafe down."

Brenda laughed. "Take no notice, Dave. We know Joe. He's trying to kid you. He's aching to get his teeth into this business. He always is."

Joe made an effort to moderate her declaration. "Well, it's

true, I don't mind helping out on these things, but you know…" He trailed off unable to conjure up more excuses.

Kane applied further pressure and for a brief moment, Joe understood why the man was the Transport Manager at Ballantynes. He had no hesitation in going after what he wanted. "If it's a question of money, don't worry. I said we'll pay whatever fee you ask."

"It's nothing to do with money. It's…" again Joe trailed off, feebly searching for anything which would make sense.

What he really wanted was to say, 'yes, I'll do it,' but there were any number of factors holding him back, not least of which was the possible complexity of the investigation and the lack of time – he had only until Sunday night, Monday morning at the latest. Joe did not like to go home to Sanford leaving investigations hanging. He preferred them solved.

He became conscious of everyone waiting for him to say something.

"It's what, Joe?" Sheila asked.

He formed the response rapidly. "I dunno. There's just something telling me to keep away from it."

Kane seized on the admission. "Look, Joe, if it's the police —"

The words clicked in Joe's mind and he cut Kane off. "That's just what it is. That Burrows, he warned me, you know. He said if he found me at your place again, he'd book me for obstructing a police investigation."

"That could make life awkward if you turn up with your driver to collect the bus on Monday morning," Kane observed.

"Exactly what I told him."

"Joe, don't worry about Chief Inspector Burrows. He will do as he's told."

Brenda almost choked on her drink. Her eyes widened and slowly swivelled to fall on Sheila, whose face had become a mask of fury. Joe noted the reactions of his friends. Like him, Brenda had read between the lines, and Sheila's reaction was to be expected. Her late husband had had a distinguished career with the police.

To head off the argument, he demanded, "Don't tell me Ballantynes own the police, too."

A rueful smile crossed Kane's lips. "Nothing of the kind. Ballantynes uphold the rule of law. We don't hide behind corporate lawyers, and if there is anything untoward in the manner of our employees' deaths, then we insist on getting to the truth."

To Joe it sounded like a prepared speech, but he resisted the temptation to applaud and call for the author. Instead, he said, "You just want to control the media. Put a bit of spin on it."

"There is that aspect," Kane agreed. "The police are not particularly subtle when it comes to dealing with the press, and as I explained before, we don't like any story that would show the company in a bad light. Burrows has already gone on record as saying it was a fight between the two men."

"And that reflects badly upon your company, Mr Kane?" Sheila hissed.

"Not so much on the company but the management, Mrs Riley. Without the full background, the press will ask what kind of management is in place at Ballantynes that could allow an argument between two individuals to get out of hand."

Sheila's furious features indicated she was about to go on the attack again. Kane read it accurately and pressed on before she could speak.

"If it could be demonstrated that the two men were killed by a third party, it wouldn't be as damning for us."

It was not the wisest thing he could have said. She put down her glass, jumped to her feet and stormed from the table.

"I'd better go after her; calm her down." With an apologetic smile, Brenda quickly followed her friend.

Kane was nonplussed. "Did I say something out of place?"

"And then some," Joe told him. "Sheila's husband was a cop. Smashing bloke, honest as the day is long. Every word you said,

Dave, came out as an attempt to manipulate the media and by insinuation, the cops."

"I won't deny that. Every large company seeks to control the media, Joe, and they exercise whatever authority they can over the police. Most of them do it covertly, using expensive lawyers to suppress information. At least I'm being honest about it."

"Dropping yourself in it, more like. Come on, Dave. What did you mean when you said Burrows would do as he was told?"

"Sir Douglas Ballantyne is not without influence, Joe. He can number the Lord Lieutenant of the County, the Police and Crime Commissioner and the Chief Constable on his list of contacts. I don't know for sure, but he will have spoken to at least one of these people, possibly all three, and he will have insisted that you be permitted to investigate. By tomorrow morning, Chief Inspector Burrows will understand that he is to co-operate with you, and keep you informed of any progress … as long as it's not breaching any confidences, of course."

"Which means he can hold back on anything."

"I understand that," Kane agreed, "but it's the best we could hope for, Joe. Naturally, one of the conditions is that you … we must keep the police informed of any information we turn up."

"I do that as a matter of routine anyway." Joe sipped at his drink. "Listen, Dave, I'm not saying no, but before I agree to take it on, you have to know what you're letting yourself in for."

Kane laughed and took a large swallow of his lemonade. "The third degree? Intense spotlights and a bad cop in my face?"

Joe smiled. "Much worse than that."

Kane's chubby features fell. He put down his glass and toyed with it, running his finger through the condensation covering the outside, watching the ice melting inside. "How do you mean?"

Feeling himself truly in control of the situation for the first time, Joe asked, "What are you going to do if I reach the same conclusions as the cops? I mean, I don't think this was a result of two men fighting, but I might be wrong. It's not entirely unknown."

Kane continued playing with his glass, his fingers working agitatedly on its exterior surface as if he were determined to remove all the condensation. "If that's the case, then so be it. I don't see what we can do other than deal with it."

"All right. Let's move on from there. Listen to me carefully, Dave, because you're not gonna like what you hear, but it's necessary."

Kane took another swallow from his glass, put it down and pushed it away, devoting his full attention to Joe.

"I'm an employer. Just like you. Not on the same scale, obviously, but I employ people." He gestured at the empty seats around them. "Sheila and Brenda, for starters, and my nephew, Lee. As their employer, I know a lot about them, but if push came to shove, no one would get that information from me without a court order. You are in the same position. You can't even tell an employee's wife his telephone number without that employee's permission."

"Absolute confidentiality," Kane agreed.

"You are going to have to breach that confidentiality where Peter Cruikshank and Stan Crowther are concerned."

Joe fell silent again, waiting for Kane's reaction.

It came in the form of a simple question. "Why?"

"In this case, as in so many others, there are no witnesses. Or at least, none that we know about. We need to understand three things: means, motive and opportunity. The first and last can usually be easily determined, but the second, motive, can be an absolute bugger to work out. The best witnesses in such cases are the dead men. I don't have any science to back me up. I use logic, and the first stage in that process is getting to know as much as I can about the men. Once we know why, we can then narrow down the suspects. I will need to know everything about them. Not only that, but I need to understand your operation, their roles within it, and I'll need to know about other members of your crew who may have a bearing on the matter. You are going to have to breach every principle of employee confidentiality. If you don't, or if you're not prepared to, then you're wasting my time, and I might just as well take it easy and enjoy my weekend in Blackpool."

Kane sucked in his breath then chewed his lip while drumming his fingers on the table. "It's asking a lot, Joe."

"The police will get round to it eventually, and they won't waste breath on it. You refuse and they'll come back with a court order. I mean it, Dave. You have to do this, or there's no point me leaving this hotel."

Kane remained silent for a full minute. To Joe it seemed as if the portly Ballantynes' man was weighing up the pros and cons of the argument. Out on the floor, the Sanford 3rd Age Club members were smooching to Chris de Burgh's *Lady in Red*, and at the bar, Sheila and Brenda were in earnest conversation, casting occasional glances at Joe. Outside, the sun had gone down, and the sky was darkening, but the lights of the North Pier called to the masses that the day's excitement was far from over, and Blackpool seafront was as busy as ever, with people milling, moving in one direction or another, yet more of them crowding the occasional, brilliantly lit tram as it passed by.

"All right, Joe. Sir Douglas places great store in trust between us and our employees, but I know what he would say if I put this to him. He would tell me to do whatever is necessary. I'll have to call the union woman in."

Joe was surprised. "Why?"

"Well, for one thing, we're talking about one of her members: Stan Crowther. We're about to divulge information on him, and she will need to be briefed and present when the information is handed over."

"I don't see—"

"That's how we work," Kane said, holding up a hand to cut Joe off. "Secondly there is the point that Amy Willows, the woman in question knows both men, Peter and Stan, as well, if not better than I do. She may be able to add to our information."

"All right," Joe agreed, "so call her in. Is she bolshie?"

"Not really. Hard line, of course, when we're coming down on one of her members, but she's quite moderate and we can usually reach agreement by consensus rather than threat and counter-threat."

"Fine." Joe changed the subject slightly. "I'll need some time to enjoy Blackpool while I'm here, Dave. So I'm not gonna give you my exclusive attention. I often find I need thinking time, anyway. But we can start in the morning, if you're all right. You working tomorrow?"

"I can arrange to be there."

"It's Easter. You have no family commitments?"

Kane shook his head. "I've been divorced a long time, Joe. The job, you know."

Thoughts of Alison leapt unbidden into Joe's head. "I know, all right. So, shall we say half ten to eleven o'clock tomorrow?"

With a nod, Kane stood up and they shook hands. "I'll be there ... oh, and don't forget to get receipts for your taxi fares."

Chapter Six

During breakfast the following morning, Joe was not much surprised to find an angry Chief Inspector Burrows enter the dining room, look around, then bear down on him.

"I want a word with you, Murray. Outside. Now."

Sat with Sheila and Brenda, Joe pointed to the empty chair to his right. "I'm having breakfast, so sit down, get a cup of tea and pick your word."

"I said I want a word with you. In private."

Joe turned on him, glowering up. "Do I look that dumb? You wanna haul me outta here, then you come with a warrant. But you don't have one, do you? Because all you're gonna do is chew me out over Ballantynes. Well anything you have to say, you can say in front of witnesses." He indicated his two friends in turn. "Sheila Riley, widow of the late Inspector Peter Riley, West Yorkshire Police, and Brenda Jump, a former senior bank clerk and widow of a colliery manager. As witnesses go, they're the best. Ladies, this is Detective Chief Inspector Burrows, one chuffed off senior investigating officer on the Ballantyne case."

"And we both know why I'm chuffed off, don't we?" Burrows retorted with a brief nod at the two women. He took the empty chair alongside Joe, picked up the teapot and helped himself. "I thought I'd made my position clear."

"You did, but—"

"Well, you ignored me and got what you wanted, Murray. You're allowed to investigate, but I'm warning you, if you find anything, you bring it to me. Withhold one tiny piece of information from me, and I'll charge you with attempting to pervert the course of justice."

"Are you finished?" Joe asked, slicing through a tough rasher of bacon, and spearing a piece with his fork. Chewing on it, he waited for Burrows to reply, but the chief inspector instead busied himself spooning sugar into his tea, and topping it up with milk.

Joe swallowed the bacon. "I didn't ask to be let in."

"Pull the other one."

"I'm telling you, I didn't. Dave Kane came here last night, and if anyone pulled strings with your Chief Constable, it was the old man who owns Ballantynes, not me. Sir Douglas."

"I don't care if it was a deputation from the House of Lords, I meant what I said. One missing piece of information and—"

"Yeah, yeah, yeah. I heard you. You'll lock me up and throw the key away." With a good deal of irritation, Joe tossed his knife and fork onto the empty plate and pushed it to the middle of the table. Topping up his tea, offering the pot to both Sheila and Brenda, who refused, he stirred his cup angrily. "I don't understand you people. You're on the telly every five minutes begging the public for help, but when it's offered, you chuck it right back."

"We don't object to help," Burrows replied. "We object to amateur bloody Poirots shoving their oar in."

"I am not an amateur bloody Poirot," Joe retorted. "Do you know anything about me?"

"Enough to be able to count the number of police officers you've made fools of."

"With the best will in the world, Chief Inspector, Joe has never made a fool of anyone," Sheila pointed out. "The police hold him in high regard in many areas of the North and Midlands."

"And he has never failed to bring them up to date on any of his investigations," Brenda added.

While addressing the two women, Burrows pointed an accusing finger at Joe. "He shoved his nose into a murder on a North Sea Ferry despite the British police's insistence that he be arrested on suspicion of that same crime."

"But you conveniently forget to mention that I was innocent." Joe retorted. "And if Captain Hagen hadn't allowed me to look into it, the real killers would have been half way to Middlesbrough while Talbot was trying to prove me guilty."

Burrows carried on talking to Sheila as if Joe had not spoken. "And forgive me, but are you the same Sheila Riley who put a chief superintendent away?"

"I am," Sheila said defiantly. "And I don't apologise for it. He murdered one of his colleagues. And, Chief Inspector, if you do your homework properly, you'll know that my late husband was a police officer. Inspector Peter Riley served for many years, and never once stepped out of line."

"Could we keep our voices down, please?" Brenda gestured around. "Right now, we're more popular than last night's disco."

Joe, too, looked around, and learned that they were, indeed the centre of attention. "It's all right, people. I'm not under arrest."

"Wait while they search your room, Joe," Alec Staines called out. "You can't keep hiding these body parts all over the country."

The remark drew a ragged laugh from the STAC members, and another look of thunder from Burrows.

"He was joking," Joe said. "Now listen, I'm not here to tread on your toes. I'd have preferred to spend the weekend enjoying myself and let you cock it up on your own, but Ballantynes have insisted. I know you have your orders, I know you're not happy about it, and to be honest, if I had to choose someone to work with, it wouldn't be you, but let's just make the best of a bad situation, huh?"

Burrows stared owlishly.

In an effort to get through to him, Joe went on, "You were convinced that Crowther and Cruikshank were fighting and accidentally killed each other. I don't see it, personally, but what persuades you."

"They had a history," the chief inspector replied. "There's been bad blood between them for years and it came to a head yesterday after Crowther hit your bus. Cruikshank suspended him."

"Crowther had been hit twice on the back of the neck, Cruikshank only once. How do you work that out?"

Burrows' tones were still grudging. "The post mortems are being carried out right now. We should have the results before the day is out. The way we see it, they carried the argument out onto the trailer park. We reckon Crowther hit Cruikshank, hard enough to stun him, but not enough to kill him instantly. Cruikshank recovered, took the weapon and hit Crowther. As he went down, Cruikshank hit him again and that killed him."

"And then Cruikshank returned to the building and made his way to security, but before he could tell us anything, he dropped dead."

"Correct. Where Crowther was found there's no coverage from the security cameras. We're chasing up a warrant so we can check the footage from other cameras in the yard."

"Why don't you just come on strong with them? You're not shy about browbeating me."

Burrows scowled. "You're not Ballantyne bloody Distribution. You don't have the same clout as them … or at least, I didn't think you had."

"For the last time, Burrows, it was nothing to do with me. I'm on my way out there in about half an hour. If I turn anything up, I'll let you know." Joe took a paper napkin and scrawled his mobile number on it. "That's me if there's anything you need to talk to me about."

Burrows took the napkin and handed over his card. "The only thing I need from you, Murray, is a goodbye wave when you're on your way home. You find anything, you ring me." He drained his cup and with a final glare, left.

"Not a candidate for your fan club, Joe," Sheila commented.

Brenda smiled. "But he'll probably enjoy dancing on your

grave."

***

Joe guessed that Amy Willows was about fifty. A good looking woman, slim and trim, but whose pretty, pear-drop face was clouded by intense anger in her blue eyes. When Kane introduced them and they shook hands, he found her grip firm, but cold and peremptory.

With the previous day's argument at the forefront of his mind, he had asked for a hi-visibility vest when he arrived at the main gate, and security guard, Dodd, had issued one. Reg Barnes had been as circumspect as he had been the day before, but had grudgingly signed Joe in with no argument, before Kane and Amy met him in reception.

After the formal introductions, Amy went straight on the attack.

"I think you should know, Mr Murray, that I disapprove of this whole business."

"What business? Murder?" Joe gave her his most disarming smile.

"You know what I'm talking about. Accessing information on one of my members. I know he's deceased, but—"

"Maybe we should discuss this in private," Joe cut in. "Not that I'm particularly bothered what your security personnel might hear, but I wouldn't want to embarrass you in front of them."

The interruption brought Amy up sharp. She glanced over Joe's shoulder to the reception counter, where Reg was ostensibly checking his logs and Sandra was studying her magazine and the CCTV screens. There was little doubt that both were listening in.

"My office, I think," Kane said. "It's quieter up there."

Kane led them through into the warehouse and towards Dispatch. As they walked, he explained the system.

"All goods are picked from the various warehouses around the site. They're labelled, and the computers read the barcodes once they're on the carousel." He pointed up at the conveyor belts circling the entire warehouse. "The trailers for our various distribution depots are always on the same bays, so when the parcel gets to its relevant bay, the computer tips the tray, the goods come down to the loaders."

They paused a moment to watch a small parcel tipped from a tray above them. It slid down a chute, and at the key point where the chute diverged to cover two loading bays, a gate swung across to direct the parcel to the correct bay. A few seconds later, it landed on the conveyor belt where it was carried into the trailer and a loader took it for stacking with other goods.

"Accurate?" Joe asked.

"One hundred percent," Kane declared as they moved off again. "We do get mistakes, yes, but they're usually found to be human errors further back in the system; picking, labelling and so on."

Reaching the far end, instead of moving into the Dispatch and drivers' rest area, they turned to the corner of the building, and through a pair of stout double doors. When the doors closed behind them, Joe noticed, as he had done the previous day, that all noise from the warehouse ceased.

They were confronted with double, glass doors leading to the outside. Both were locked and barred. Through them Joe could see some of the tractor units parked up in lines.

"Emergency exit," Kane explained. "In case of fire. Otherwise, they're kept locked. The only official way in and out of this building is through the security exit, passing through the scanner."

To the left was a flight of stone steps. Joe looked up and saw that it turned its way through several flights, to the top of the building.

"Staircase access to all three floors," Kane told him. "Now, if we go back, we can take the lift up to—"

"No," Joe interrupted. "Let's take the stairs instead." He looked over Kane's portly figure. "You up to it?"

Kane laughed. "I have to do it when there's a fire drill, Joe. Mind you, that's usually coming down."

Joe smiled. "We're not in a rush."

"Just a minute, Mr Murray—" Amy began, only to be cut off again.

"Please call me Joe."

"Whatever. You said we'll talk somewhere private. Well no one can hear us here."

Joe looked up the stairs. "Better up there."

He led the way, but he scanned every individual step, and the surrounding walls as they made their way up the flights of stairs, until they reached the third floor where the staircase came to an end on a broad landing, leaving them confronted with the familiar double doors to one side, and a window with panoramic views across the site, on the other.

He noticed that irritation was the key feature for Amy, and puzzlement had troubled Kane throughout the slow, tortuous journey, but Kane was too out of breath to ask, and Amy appeared as if she still did not trust Joe enough to speak to him.

Ignoring the view of sunshine through the window, Joe ran a practiced eye over the walls. To the right of the doors, he spotted something on the wall, and examined it close up.

"Have the police forensic people been up here?" he asked.

"No," Kane replied, still gasping for breath. "Well, that is, Burrows has, but he didn't order any examination of the area. He came for Peter's mobile phone. That's all."

"What is it?" Amy asked.

Keeping his finger away from the area, Joe pointed it out. "Scuff mark. And it looks like a hair attached to it. That would indicate maybe a bit of blood just tacking it to the wall."

"It could have been there years," Kane pointed out.

"It could. Or it could have been lodged there yesterday. Let's see what we can learn, eh?" Joe stood back and allowed Kane to lead them through into the third floor warehouse, and along to his office.

Light and roomy were the first thoughts that struck Joe. One side lined with windows looking out onto the north yard, while the remainder was taken up with one large desk, and two smaller tables pushed together. A line of filing cabinets stood against the back wall, and above them, was a shelf holding box files. A large map of the United Kingdom with the local distribution depots flagged up by coloured pins sat above the desk. Joe was tempted to count them, but the bunching of many pins in major centres of population would have made the task impossible.

Joe and Amy took opposite sides of the tables, while Kane busied himself on the phone for a few moments. At length, putting the receiver down, he took a seat between and at right angles to them.

"I've asked for some tea," he reported.

"Good. Soon as it's delivered, we can get down to business."

Amy, who had been quietly seething sine thy left the security station, let rip. "I think I've waited long enough. You are about to examine records of one of my members, and I object to that in the strongest possible terms. It's a breach of confidentiality and I refuse to set a precedent."

Joe smiled thinly. "Years ago, a salesman told me that the key to controlling a conversation is not just answering objections, but choosing *when* to answer them."

"And that's what this is about, is it? Control?"

"No. I think he was talking through his hat. But then, I'm not trying to sell you anything. I am going to take another leaf out of that salesman's book, and ask you questions, the first one being, do you believe that Peter Cruikshank and Stan Crowther beat other to death?"

Her face was a picture of defiance. "I do not."

"Why?"

73

The question threw her momentarily, but when she eventually answered it was in measured, certain tones. "I knew them both. I've known them for twenty odd years. They antagonised each other, certainly, but the company is quite strict on violence. Any employee caught fighting is liable for summary dismissal… no exceptions. Both Peter and Stanley had far too much to lose to be caught like that. They had their set-to's, yes, but if it came to blows, and I don't believe it did, it would have been handbags. Nothing more."

"Right. I didn't know either man, so I can't comment on your superior knowledge, but I have other reasons for believing Burrows has it wrong. I don't think they killed each other, either."

"So we're have some measure of agreement," Amy said, "but that doesn't make it right to let you check their records."

"I don't want to check their records, and I never did," Joe told her.

Her eyes widened and Joe paused to let the surprise sink in.

With a generous smile at Kane, Joe went on, "What I actually said to Dave lost something in translation. I said I needed to know everything about the two men, and gathering that information will breach confidentiality rules. But I don't want to see their employment records. They'd tell me nothing anyway. Instead, I want to *know* about them. I'm asking you and Dave, as the people who, so I'm told, knew them best, to tell me everything about them. Every tiny little thing. Don't leave anything out. Do you think you can do that, Amy?"

Thrown slightly by his manoeuvring, she nodded. "I'll tell you what I can."

"Good." Joe checked his watch and read 11:15. "Where's this tea coming from, Dave? Darjeeling?"

Kane laughed. "Dispatch. It shouldn't be long."

"Well, while we're waiting, let's get on." Joe took out his notebook and pen. "Burrows told me that you said there was a long history of bad blood between Peter and Stan."

"That's right," Kane agreed. "It goes back … oh … ten years?" He looked to Amy for agreement and she nodded.

"What was at the root of it?" Joe demanded.

Both looked uncomfortable, and neither was in a hurry to reply.

"Two guys don't just decide to hate each other," Joe pressed, "so there's obviously something in the past that set them against one another. As colleagues you must know what it's all about."

"I'm, er, I'm not sure it's relevant," Kane said. "It has nothing to do with Ballantynes."

Disbelief caused Joe to raise his voice. "Nothing to do with … according to the cops, they got into a fight and killed each other on your premises. I'd say that makes it a lot to do with Ballantynes. Now listen, Dave, we have an agreement. You ask me to help, I said yes, but I need to know everything which may be pertinent, and whatever the beef between these two, it's pertinent, even if it's only to lead the law up the wrong garden path. Now either fill me in, or I'll walk out of here and go back to enjoying my weekend off."

A silence followed. It was probably only a matter of a few seconds, but to Joe it seemed like an age. Kane and Amy exchanged a single glance, but then would not look at each other. They found the barren walls of the office or the bland brown of the carpet tiles more interesting.

There was a knock on the door and Megan Stafford entered carrying a tray of tea things.

Joe recognised her and beamed a smile of greeting on her. "You okay today, luv?" he asked.

"Much better, thanks."

She placed the tea tray on the table and left them.

"She was very upset yesterday afternoon," Joe told the others.

"Must have been the shock, then." Amy said. "She didn't care for either Stan or Peter."

Joe made a mental note of it.

Amy and Kane appeared to have found some relief from the

interruption, and they busied themselves pouring tea, sorting out milk and sugar, and furnishing Joe and themselves with refreshments.

And while he watched the innocuous antics, Joe's irritation grew. They enjoyed the distraction; it took their minds away from the direct and disturbing question he had asked. While he waited for them to settle again, he racked his brain to ascertain what could be so damning that it called for such recalcitrance.

"Right, so we have tea and biscuits. Now tell me what the hell was going on between these two guys."

He was greeted with another silence, shorter this time, while unspoken messages passed between the pair, each willing the other to deliver the story.

Joe was about to step up his demand, when Kane said, "I think it would be better coming from you, Amy."

She gave the briefest of nods, and then spent a few moments looking through the windows. Joe followed her stare and focussed on the upper arches of The Big One. He had the feeling that whatever was to come, it affected her in the same way that the rollercoaster affected its passengers. Thrilling, yet frightening.

Eventually, she took a breath and began.

"Peter and Stanley were the best of friends. They met while they were in the army, and they became pals. When they got out, Stan landed a job here as a driver. He managed to get Peter a job, too, so within three months, they were both working for Ballantynes as drivers. Stan was on days, Peter on nights, and recognising their friendship, the company made them tractor buddies."

Joe frowned. "Tractor buddies?"

Kane took up the explanation. "The company realised a long time ago, Joe, that if you keep the same driver on a tractor unit, he looks after it. He keeps it clean inside and out, and he reports the smallest of problems. He tends to have fewer bumps and scrapes because he's living in it for one third of his life."

"Logical enough," Joe agreed. "I deal with plenty of truckers at my café."

"The difficulty is we run twenty-four-seven," Kane went on. "Which means you have a man driving a tractor on days and a different man on nights. The company decided that we would use the same two men on a tractor all the time, or at least, as close to all the time as we could. They were tractor buddies."

"The system worked," Amy said. "They took care of their tractors, and any unreported knocks or bumps could be narrowed down to one of two men, and that made the drivers aware of the need to report such incidents. It would get them into a flaming argument with their tractor buddy if they didn't."

"I get the idea," Joe said. "So Stan and Peter were tractor buddies."

"Correct. Stan would start at seven in the morning and be finished for six in the evening. Before he clocked off, he would wash the tractor exterior and clean the interior. He'd check it over, report anything that needed reporting or, if he had a situation where he needed to book the unit off for repairs, he would do so. Peter came on duty at seven in the evening and finished at six in the morning, and he would go through exactly the same routine. It was good system. It reduced the amount of time tractors spent off the road."

"Okay, so I'm clued up. What went wrong?"

"Their lifestyles were different," Amy replied. "Peter was married. He met his wife here at Ballantynes, and it's why he worked nights. What with children, a mortgage and other commitments, he needed the extra money. Stan hated the thought of marriage." She smiled fondly. "He always said his worst nightmare would be waking up to find that he was married."

The connections began to form in Joe's mind. "I think I can see where this is going, but carry on."

Amy sighed again. "The inevitable happened, as I think you've guessed. Stan would finish work at six, Peter started at seven, and by half past nine, Stan was in bed with Peter's wife."

Joe tutted. "With friends like that, you don't need to go shopping for enemies, do you? And Peter found out, did he?"

Amy nodded. "It had been going on six months when someone tipped him the wink. Peter played it very clever. He booked a night off, but he asked the managers here to keep it secret. He turned up for work as usual, but his job was handed to a temp driver, while Peter went home. He sat in the lane, not far from his house until he saw Stan's car pass. Then he gave his wife and Stan half an hour before walking up to the house and caught them at it on the front room rug."

Joe shook his head sadly. "End of friendship."

"More than that, Joe. It wrecked Peter's marriage. Stan didn't want to know the wife, Peter couldn't forgive her, so they all ended up living alone and all ended up very angry at each other."

Joe seized on the statement. "Hold on. So here we have a wife who's been a bloody fool, and she's lost everything. She's angry at Stan because he doesn't want her, she's angry at Peter because he doesn't want her either, and she's probably angry at herself for behaving like a bitch on heat. She worked here, too, you said. Is it possible that the resentment could have built up until yesterday when she snapped and went for both men?"

"No," Kane said. "All this was ten years ago, Joe."

"Yes but—"

"I can assure you, Peter's ex-wife had no part in this," Amy interrupted.

Her confidence irritated Joe. "How do you know?"

"Because I am Peter's ex-wife."

Chapter Seven

Joe felt as if he should have second-guessed where Amy was heading, and he was irritated that he had not seen her admission coming. He took his annoyance out on her. "And that's why you didn't want to talk about it?" he demanded. "Embarrassment?"

"Partly," Amy confessed. "It's an open secret. Everyone who's been with Ballantynes for any length of time knows about it, but no one speaks of it. Listen, Joe, I hold a senior position within the union here. I've been with the company for almost thirty years. Ever since I left school. The only time I had off, aside from holidays, was maternity leave. You think I want people sniggering behind my back? You think I want drivers and loaders hitting on me because they think I'm easy? I know what I did. I know it was wrong. Peter and I tried to patch it up, but he couldn't. If it had been anyone but Stan, maybe, but they were best friends, and the unwritten law says you don't do that to your best friend. I mean, are you married?"

Joe shook his head. "Divorced. A long time now. But there was no one else involved. We just didn't see eye to eye, businesswise." He paused a moment, marshalling his thoughts. "Look, you insist this had nothing to do with the incident yesterday. How can you be sure? All right, so it's ten years ago, but Peter could still have harboured a lot of resentment."

"And he did," Amy promptly agreed.

Kane tutted and Joe turned his attention to the manager, raising his eyebrows to invite comment.

"Peter was always better motivated than Stan," Kane declared. "Stan was quite happy to remain a driver. Peter was more ambitious, so while he was still driving he took management courses and got the necessary qualifications to bring him off the road into the office. The CPC, Certificate of Professional Competence."

"I've heard it mentioned," Joe said. "Remember, I run a truckstop."

"Yes, well, within two years of Amy and Peter splitting up, Peter was promoted. He began as an assistant in Dispatch, and he applied himself. About three years ago, he became my deputy."

"And he made life hell for Stan."

Joe spotted the look of fury crossing Kane's face, but before he could comment, Amy got there.

"I'm sorry, Dave, but facts are facts. I've been researching this all week, and the figures show that Peter came down harder on Stan than he did any other driver. For minor infringements, most drivers would get a telling off, but Stan would get a formal warning. Peter would take the first opportunity to cut Stan's safe driving bonus."

"Safe driving bonus? Joe frowned. "They get extra money for doing what they should do anyway?"

"Welfare and productivity, Joe," Kane explained. "If a driver gets through a year with less than a set amount of repair costs, he gets a bonus of a hundred pounds. We wouldn't dock it for, say, a broken light, but more serious damage would automatically lose a driver his bonus."

"If someone hit your truck," Amy said, taking up the thread, "it wouldn't count against you, but in Stan's case it did. I've had several meetings with you over it, Dave, and you know I have."

"Amy, you're not the only one who's been looking at the stats this week. I have, too, and yes I've noticed Peter was a little hard on Stan, but have you looked into the grief Stan caused for Peter? He went out of his way to embarrass the man." Kane stood up and crossed the room to the filing cabinets. Stretching over them, standing on tiptoes, he reached up to the shelf above and dragged down a box file.

Joe noticed that the effort had cost him. He was sweating and short of breath when he got back to the table.

"Bloody idiot builders," he grumbled. "Why don't they position these shelves for someone who's only five foot three?"

Joe laughed. "I have a similar problem in my kitchen. It's a stretch to reach the top pie rack. I leave it to my nephew, these days. He's six foot and then some."

Kane grunted and opened the box file. Inside, it was crammed with what looked like official report forms. "Formal complaints from Peter concerning Stan's attitude. If something went wrong, and Stan heard about it, he'd be crowing in the dispatch office, saying things like, 'It's what you get when you have a man like him running the job.'"

"The 'him' in question being Peter?" Joe asked.

Kane nodded in passing, but his words were directed at Amy. "Stan made Peter's life hell. He compromised the man's authority."

"Is it any wonder?" Amy demanded. "Peter tried to walk all over him at every opportunity."

"People—"

To Joe's irritation, they carried on bickering, talking over his attempted interjection.

"You cannot have workers dictating to their managers. That's why you and I meet so often. If Stan had turned up at the disciplinary meeting next week, this would have all come out."

"Can we stick to the—"

Again Joe was unable to complete his demand as Amy stabbed back at Kane. "And what action would you have taken against Peter?"

"You sound as if you're on Stan's side. Against your ex-husband."

"I'm being professional, Dave. I'm paid to represent Stan's interest. My personal feelings don't enter into it. I—"

A loud CRACK cut her off. It was Joe, slamming the flat of

his hand down hard on the table top.

Silence fell and Joe glared from one to the other. "I didn't come here to listen to you two arguing office politics. Can we stick to business?" He allowed a second silence to fill the room while they brought their feelings under control. "Thank you. Okay, so we have two men constantly at each other's throats, and it's small wonder that Burrows came to the conclusion he did. Let's play it his way for a minute, and ask why should it happen yesterday? What was so special about yesterday that everything came to a head?"

"Stan was fired," Amy declared.

"Not fired; suspended," Kane argued.

"It amounts to the same thing. You would have called him back next week, and we both know he would have been sacked."

"If sufficient doubt could be established, we would have found him alternative employment," Kane retorted. "You know the company position on staff welfare. We don't—"

"You're doing it again," Joe interrupted. "Staff welfare may or may not be important to you, but it doesn't matter a toss to me. Why would Stan have been fired?"

"You know why," Kane replied. "He was drunk. He hit your bus, didn't he?"

"Ah. Right. Tell me what happened when he got back here."

"Stan was held at the gate pending the police turning up."

"And that's another thing we have to take up, Dave," Amy said. "You allowed Terry Dodd, a security man, to move that rig into the yard from the gate. He has no licence, and company rules clearly state that all drivers must hold a current HGV—"

"It was an emergency, Amy," Kane interrupted. "The rig was blocking the gate and I had to do something. Alf Sclater took almost ten minutes to get there. We couldn't have it blocking the gate like that."

"You're doing it again," Joe warned before the argument could develop further. "Getting sidetracked. Let's stick to

Crowther and Cruikshank, huh? So you had the cops take him away, Dave? What then?"

"To be frank, Joe, he was so drunk he didn't make much sense," Amy said. "I went across to the gate to stay with him until the police turned up. They breathalysed him, it was positive and they took him away. He asked me to put his bag in his locker, after which I went to the police station to collect him. By the time I got there, they'd charged him. They haven't given us precise details. They won't know until the official analysis comes back, but he was at least three times over the limit."

Kane's features darkened. "He was hammered, to put no finer point on it."

Joe stopped taking notes and frowned. "So how did Peter become involved in this?"

"He didn't. Not then, anyway," Kane explained. "Amy brought Stan back about one o'clock, and by then he was sober enough for us to hold a reasonable discussion with him."

"I took him upstairs, to this office where we met with Dave, and the management witness was Peter." Amy sighed. "And that's when it all kicked off."

***

The moment Amy and Crowther returned from the police station, they were due to meet with Kane and Cruikshank in the managers' third floor office.

Amy was angry. Like Kane, she had become tired of the constant bickering between Crowther and Cruikshank, and now it seemed that all the years of fighting were to come to nothing.

The journey from the police station, through the main entrance at Ballantynes, and through the Sort Centre was largely silent. Once inside, in a desperate, last-minute effort to sober Crowther up, they took the stairs rather than the lift, and

Amy finally decided it was time to let him know how she felt.

Her voice echoing around the empty staircase, she growled, "Three times over the limit. That's what the cops say. It's a sackable offence, Stan. There's no way I can get you out of it."

"I haven't been drinking," he insisted, his voice still slightly slurry.

"Then how do you explain the breathalyser result?

"I don't ... don't know. But it's not me." Out of breath, he had to pause at the first landing. While he leaned on the stair rail getting his breath back, his face screwed into a mask of intense concentration. "Did you ... did you put my bag in my locker?"

"Yes."

"We'll need it."

Suspicion grew across Amy's hardened features. "Why?"

"Be ... because I've know what happened, and it's that ... that *git*, Cruikshank. Your ex-bloody husband. He's fine ... finally got his own back after all these ... these years."

At once horrified and intrigued, Amy demanded. "What are you talking about?"

"You'll see. Let's just get my bag from my locker."

She listened to his explanation, and with fresh determination, dug into her pockets and came out with his locker key. "You wait here. I'll go for it." She hurried back down the stairs.

Five minutes later, with Amy carrying the black, sports holdall, they stepped into Kane's office where the management duo was already seated in the far corner of the room, their backs to the wall. Amy and Crowther took their seats. Crowther declined coffee and broke out a bottle of water, and Kane opened proceedings.

"The company position on this matter is quite clear. Excess alcohol, in this case proven by the police, warrants summary dismissal. It's my job to find out if there are extenuating circumstances, and before we go any further, I'm telling you now, it's almost impossible for there to be any."

"Dave—"

Kane cut Crowther off before he could say more. "Stan, what the hell are you playing at? You've done thousands of pounds worth of damage to other vehicles, you're facing a huge fine, possible imprisonment, you're going to lose your licence and your job, and you're dragging this company's name and reputation through the mud."

"I have not had a drink," Crowther declared.

"Then how do you account for the police findings?" Cruikshank retorted. "The breathalyser lit up like a bloody traffic light, man. And it's not just the breathalyser. " He sorted through the papers before him. "Your urine sample says you were at least three times over the limit, and they're waiting on the blood analysis, but they expect it to confirm their findings. You were blathered."

"You know, I've just about had it up to here, today," Crowther fumed. "Those idiots on security held me up for nearly ten minutes for a cab search on the way out, and now this. I'll tell you again. I have not had a drink."

Kane threw his hands up and let them fall to the table. "You're being obstructive, Stan, and you leave me no alternative. I'm sorry, but you're fired. Collect your personal belongings and I'll arrange for you to be escorted off the site."

A sly smile crept across Crowther's face. "I wouldn't do that if I were you, Dave. I said I haven't had a drink. Obviously I have, but we need to think about how I came to take a drink without my knowing about it."

Having watched the brief exchanges, Amy remained firm and determined when she spoke. "Stan insists that someone has tampered with his flask."

Cruikshank laughed; a short, sharp bark of utter derision.

"I'm not stupid," Crowther insisted. "Twenty-five years I've been here. When have you ever known me turn up for work drunk? Never. When have you ever known me take a drink

85

while I'm working? Never." He jabbed a pointing finger into the table top. "Someone fooled around with my flask of coffee and put strong alcohol in it. And we all know who." The finger lifted and aimed straight at Cruikshank. "You."

Whatever humour Cruikshank had enjoyed, faded rapidly, to be replaced by indignation. "Don't talk so soft, man."

"Yes you did, and you know you did. You've never got over me giving one to her." He jerked his thumb sideways at Amy. "You've been hell bent on getting even ever since, but you can't face me like a man, can you? So you go the crafty way about it, coming down harder on me than other drivers, making my life hell, and now this. Spiking my coffee. Well I've got the proof right here, Cruikshank, and this time, you're the one who's gonna be nailed."

"You're talking out of your backside," Cruikshank turned to his manager for support. "Dave, this is just a ruse to try and get him off the hook. Boot him out."

Kane held up a hand for silence and looked to Amy.

Slightly miffed at the way Crowther had referred to her in such an offhand manner, Amy was nevertheless anxious to get her member off the hook, but equally careful not to lay the blame with her ex-husband. "I don't know, Dave. What Stan says makes sense, but whether Peter is responsible, I really can't say."

"Bloody typical of you, that, isn't it?" Cruikshank grumbled. "Take his side."

"I'm paid to take Stan's side, Peter. Even if he's in the wrong."

"There's a simple way to settle this," Kane said. "Do you have you flask, Stan?"

"In the bag." Crowther nodded at the holdall.

"Give it to me. Even if it's empty, there'll be dregs in there, and I'll have them checked for traces of alcohol."

Crowther nodded, Amy picked up the bag and unzipped it.

It was a mess. There were notebooks, pens, an mp3 player, glossy magazines, a copy of the company schedules and his work rota, the morning newspaper, work gloves, woollen gloves, even a spare baseball cap, but there was no sign of a thermos. She looked to Crowther, and shrugged before passing him the bag.

He, too, rooted through it before tossing it to the floor. "Aw, great. Now someone's been through my gear and nicked the flask." He glowered at Cruikshank. "It's you again, isn't it? You waited while the cops hauled me off and then went into my locker to get rid of the flask, cos you knew what it would prove."

Cruikshank sneered. "Will you listen to yourself, Crowther? You're raving."

"And you're gonna pay for this." Crowther half rose.

"Calm down, Stan," Amy ordered. She waited until he was seated again. "Is there any danger you could have left the flask in your cab?"

He did not answer immediately, and she could see that he was quietly simmering away.

"Stan?"

"Mebbe. I dunno."

"When did you get your bag from the cab?" Kane asked.

"That bloody security guard got it. Dodd. He wouldn't let me back in the cab after he spoke to you. So I asked him to get my gear out, and he did. Then, when Amy came over to the gatehouse, I gave it to her and I gave her my locker key, to put it away while I went with the filth." He raised his voice and pointed a quivering finger at Cruikshank. "And he went into my locker and took the flask."

Cruikshank was also on the point of losing his temper. "You're a nutter, you are. I don't know about sacked, you should be—"

"It's common knowledge that management have keys for all the lockers," Crowther cut in. "For two pins, I'd knock you all over this yard."

"Any time you fancy your chances, pal," Cruikshank retorted

getting to his feet.

Crowther rose again. "How about right now? Come on then, big shot. Let's see—"

"Please," Amy interrupted. "We're not children." Silence fell, and she addressed Kane. "Could we check whether the flask is in the cab?"

"Of course," the manager agreed. "The minute we're done here." He switched his attention to Crowther. "Even if we find the flask, Stan, and we learn that it was, er, spiked, it doesn't change much. You should have been aware that your judgement was impaired, and you should have stopped and slept it off, or called in so we could send a relief out. The police should have made you aware that there is no defence in law, even if there may be mitigating circumstances. That said, there's obviously some doubt about what's really happened, so for the time being, I'm suspending you from duty. You'll be on full pay pending a disciplinary hearing, and that will be called within the next ten days."

"Dave—"

"I don't want to hear it, Stan," Kane interrupted. "I don't want to hear anything from you until such time as you attend the hearing. For now, I want you to collect your belongings and go home. Amy will keep you posted on progress and she'll advise you of the date of the hearing." Kane smiled briefly on the union woman. "Amy?"

"Fine. I'll have to put a report into the branch office, but I'll make sure Stan goes home first."

"Thank you."

Amy and Crowther stood. The driver picked up his holdall, and delivered a final glare at Cruikshank. "I'll get you for this. I'll put you in a wheelchair for life."

Cruikshank remained implacably confident. "Any time you like."

***

Joe made a final note and then spent a moment reading through them.

"I assume you've told the police all of this," he asked, and was greeted by nods from both Kane and Amy. Concentrating on the woman, he went on, "So you left the meeting with Crowther. What happened then?"

"I took him down to the rest room. I was supposed to escort him to the main gate, but he said he wanted to clear out his locker first. I left him there, went back to my office to type up my report, and I was there for the rest of the afternoon ... or at least until the deaths of both men spread on the grapevine, a good hour or more later."

Joe spun his head to face Kane. "And you, Dave?"

"I spent a few minutes with Peter, then went to Maintenance and the workshops to check the tractor unit, see if Stan's flask was in there. That's where I'd been when I came into the building and met you and your driver."

Joe smiled. "Not checking our bus, then?"

Kane returned the smile. "No. Not checking your bus. I'm sorry, Joe, but I couldn't tell you what I'd been doing. It was none of your business, so I just made an excuse."

"No worries. And what about Peter?"

Kane shrugged. "He was in this office when I left, and he was still here when I came back."

"And when you came back, did he appear all right?"

"Well, not really. He seemed distracted; worried. Mind you, Joe, to be fair, I had warned him that if I learned he really had tampered with Stan's flask, he'd be for the high jump, too. Legally, Stan had no defence, but if it could be proven that Peter had spiked his coffee, then that's just as criminal, and the company would ensure that not only would he lose his job, but he'd be reported to the police."

Leaning back in his seat, cradling a cup of tea in his hands, Joe considered his next point. "You know, I've been in the catering trade all my life. I have those customers who've been coming into my café for the last quarter of a century, and if there was anything wrong with the tea, they'd notice it instantly. I would, too. So what I don't understand is how come Stan didn't notice his coffee was spiked. He should have taste the booze right away."

"Not necessarily," Amy disagreed. "Stan was a sugar addict. He took anything up to four or five sugars in a cup of tea or coffee, so God knows how many he put in a flask. If someone added a strong spirit, Polish vodka, or even antifreeze, he may not have noticed it through the sugar."

"Ah." Joe sat forward and scrawled 'sugar addict' on his notepad, then leaned back again. "So what do you two think? Could his coffee have been spiked?"

Kane shrugged. Amy was more definite.

"It's not beyond the bounds of possibility. We all knew Stan. He liked a beer of an evening, but he didn't drink at work, and he knew he was on duty early doors yesterday, so he wouldn't have gone out on the beer Thursday night. Even if he did, there would be some alcohol still in his bloodstream, but not that amount. Everything points to him having taken in a lot of alcohol yesterday morning."

"And assuming someone really did meddle with his thermos, would Peter have had the opportunity?" Joe asked.

As before, Kane remained non-committal, but Amy was more certain.

"Yes, he would. Stan came in at four a.m. for a routine delivery in Sunderland and a collection in Middlesbrough. But the Sunderland delivery was cancelled late on Thursday night. Dispatch arranged for a driver from our York depot to handle the Middlesbrough collection and when Stan came in, he was put on standby, which basically means sitting in the rest room and twiddling his thumbs until a job came up. Peter started at six thirty, and was on duty until four thirty in the afternoon. At seven, Stan was given a job. A collection in Manchester; Trafford Park. Pick up a load of flatpack furniture. Now I know that job. You turn up, open the back doors, back onto the loading bay and sit in your cab until the trailer is loaded. It takes about an hour, hour and a half. I also know Stan. He would have been in the cab, drinking coffee and reading his porno magazines."

"Analysis of his tachograph shows he got to Manchester at about eight fifteen and left at about nine forty-five," Kane confirmed. "He'd had ninety minutes of gulping down coffee. So if it was spiked, it meant he took in a lot of alcohol in a short space of time."

Again Joe scrawled a few notes. "We now know that Peter had a small window of opportunity in which to spike Stan's coffee..." He trailed off as Amy opened her mouth to protest, but Joe cut her off before she could speak. "I'm not saying he did it, Amy, just that he had the chance to do it. Here's the thing I don't understand. Stan is sat in the rest room for, what? Three hours? If he was drinking out of the flask all that time, he must have been drunk before he set off, and if he wasn't then it's reasonable to assume the alcohol got into his system after he left, which points at him having a bottle with him."

Amy shook her head. "Not so. Do you know anything about truckers?"

"Only what I've learned from serving them six days a week."

"Then you should know that when a driver sets off, he never really knows when he's going to get back. An accident, traffic jams, police or ministry spot checks; it all means he can never make more than an intelligent guess at the journey time. That being the case, most of them don't use a flask in the rest room. They save it for when they're out on the road. Instead, they use the vending machines."

Joe considered the explanation, found it satisfactory and made a note. "Dave, you went to the tractor unit to see if the flask was in there. Was it?"

"No."

"You were carrying something weighty in the pockets of your

91

hi-vis coat when you met us in reception, and I noticed something sticking out of your jacket pocket yesterday. A sort of wrist loop."

Kane did not appear offended by the insinuation. "It was a torch. The lighting in the workshop is good, but not that good, and those cabs tend to be dark. I needed the flashlight to have a good look round. The flask was not in there."

Joe recalled seeing a heavy duty flashlight on Terry Dodd's belt the previous day. "Fair enough. Amy, you went to the locker to collect Stan's bag. Was the flask in the locker?"

"No. I'm sure I would have noticed if it were."

"All right. Final question, for now. Is it true that management have keys to the lockers?"

"No," Kane said. "Security have them and, of course, the drivers have them, but we don't."

"Not the final question, then," Joe corrected himself. "Why do security have keys?"

"You know about our search rules, Joe," Kane explained. "Everyone is liable to be searched on entry and exit to the site."

Joe was appalled. "You can be searched coming in?"

"Yes. It doesn't happen often, but you are liable to have your vehicle searched as you come into the yard and again when you leave. That search right extends to locker rooms. Now and then senior management, those above us, will order a full search, and security have to open the lockers."

"There are strict protocols, Joe," Amy said, taking up the tale. "Lockers cannot be opened without either the owner or his-stroke-her union representative and a member of the management staff, either Dave or Peter or one of the senior people in Dispatch, being present. Forgive me, but you seem to be making quite a lot of this."

"I am," Joe admitted, "but it's because Burrows will when he gets his act together. Tell me something, both of you. What time did you turn up for work yesterday?"

"Half past eight," Amy replied.

"I was here for about nine," Kane confirmed.

"So unless you had sneaked in earlier, neither of you could have tampered with Stan's flask because by the time you got here, he was gone, on his way to Manchester. And if you did sneak in earlier, it would show up in the security logs somewhere along the line. But I'm not so concerned with who spiked the coffee. The obvious culprit is Peter … no, no, hear me out, Amy. I'm not accusing, simply stating the obvious. Right now, I'm more concerned with what happened to the flask later, and there are four possibilities. One, Stan had done the dirty on himself, whether by design or accident, and he got rid of the flask. It doesn't seem likely, but it's a possibility. Two, Peter spiked the drink, and later, while Stan was at the police station, he went to the locker and removed the evidence. Three, you, Dave, found the flask in the tractor unit and disposed of it, and four, you, Amy, got rid of it when you went down to collect Stan's bag."

Chapter Eight

Like the day before when he had announced Cruikshank's death as murder, Joe rode out the inevitable protests, silently formulating his response while Amy and Kane took turns to curse and castigate him.

When silence fell, Kane was left red-faced and sweating, Amy simply red-faced with anger, and Joe took up the reins again.

"Let's look at the reality of the situation, huh? Because if I don't, Burrows and his people will, and at some point, they'll drag you both to the station for questioning. The business between Peter and Stan has been going on for about ten years, so you say. And who's to blame? When you boil it all down, who is the real guilty party? Stan. All right, Amy, so you fell for his charms, whatever they were, but if you're no pushover, and I assume you're not, then it means he pursued you. We all know it takes at least two to party, but would you still be married to Peter if Stan had not seduced you?"

Her answer was reluctant, filled with bitterness. "Possibly. Probably. I don't know."

"And you, Dave. You tell me that Peter was your natural successor, your protégé, but Stan consistently undermined his authority, and you spent a lot of time in meetings with Amy and Stan trying to smooth things out. So if you had to get rid of one man, who would it be? Peter or Stan? The answer, so it seems to me, is Stan. Get rid of him and everything falls into place."

"Joe, I'm the boss. There are ways and means of getting people out from under your hair without killing them."

Joe screwed up his face. Do you mean out from under your feet, or out of your hair?"

"You know what I'm talking about," Kane rasped.

"All right, I know. But I'm not talking about the death of either man. I'll come to that eventually. Right now, I'm talking about Stan getting tanked up, and how that may have come about." He fell silent, again mentally forming his words. "Let me paint you a picture. Like you, Peter has had enough of Stan, so he needs to find a way of getting rid of him. The opportunity presents itself yesterday morning, so he sneaks strong alcohol into Stan's flask, then sends him on his way to a collection in Manchester where he knows Stan will be idle for at least an hour... no, no, hear me out, Amy."

Again he paused so she could back off and listen.

"Peter's plan is simple. Stan will get drunk on the coffee, and ring in for a relief driver to come and bring the rig back here. At that point, Stan will face disciplinary action for being drunk on duty. You may sack him, but even if you didn't, even if you just relocated him to another department, he's still out of Peter's hair and yours. But it all goes wrong when Stan drives the truck back, does a lot of damage to other vehicles on the motorway and the police are called in. Worse than that, there will be a preliminary hearing and Peter knows Stan will accuse him. He has to get that flask and get rid of it before it can incriminate him. So he approaches you, Dave, or you, Amy, and confesses. After a bit of argument, he persuades one of you to help him. Either you, Dave, got rid of the flask over in the workshop, or you, Amy, removed it from Stan's locker. Stan has no proof, he's on his way out, one of you has a useful hold over Peter, and everyone is happy... except Stan, but who gives a damn about him?"

Joe fell silent again, waiting for their response. When it came, it was from Kane, and it was remarkably mild.

"It didn't happen, Joe."

Satisfied, Joe said, "I didn't say it did. I said it was a theory.

Trust me on this, Burrows may be a grumpy copper, but he's not thick. He can't be to get to his level. He will come round to this eventually, and unless we have alternative ideas, he will pursue it."

"So how do we prove we're innocent?" Amy demanded.

"We find the flask." Joe gave his suggestion a little more thought. "Mind you, even if we find it, it's not conclusive. Unless you were wearing gloves, your dabs will be all over it, but let's say your prints aren't on it? If it's been wiped clean, say, then that supports the theory and you could have a tough time explaining it away."

"Great," Kane grumbled. "We have nothing to do with it, but we get accused just the same."

Joe smiled. "I've been there. I was accused of strangling a woman last year. Not only one, but two. I'd a hell of a job proving it wasn't me, but I got there in the end."

"Two?" Amy gaped.

"It was a deliberate attempt to frame me, and the killer made enough mistakes for me to solve the case." Joe laughed. "It happens. Especially when your name's Joe Murray. Now come on. We need to move on and concentrate on the actual killings."

Kane looked confused. "We know nothing about them, Joe. All I saw is what you saw yesterday, and I'm sure Amy was in her office all afternoon."

"You know a lot more than me," Joe replied. "You just don't know you know it yet. We need to think about the timescale. Y'see, it's very difficult for a pathologist to establish time of death with any great accuracy. They make educated guesses based on a number of factors. Now in this case, we know exactly what time Peter died. We were there. What we don't know is the time Stan died. If Burrows is right, then it was before Peter was killed. If Burrows is wrong, then it's all up in the air. It could still be before, but it could also be after. The post mortem will not be able to narrow down the time of death that closely, so it's all about who saw whom, what, where and when. Now, Amy, you were with Stan after the meeting. What time did you leave him?"

"About ten past two."

"And at that time, you say he was clearing out his locker."

"Yes. He was obviously expecting the sack."

"Is that one of those lockers I saw in the drivers' rest room?"

"Yes."

Joe switched his attention to Kane. "Dave, you spent a few minutes talking to Peter after the meeting, and then you went to the workshops. What time did you leave Peter?"

"Like Amy, it would have been about ten past two."

"And you got back to security at about twenty to three. I know because I was there. After speaking with Keith and myself, you went to get your forms and you say you returned to this office, where you saw Peter. What time would that be?"

"As near as I can guess, about ten to three."

"And Peter was alive then, as we know. But was Stan?" Joe strummed his lips thoughtfully. "Let's assume he took another five minute to clear out his locker, and then left the building. That would be a quarter past two. Dave, while you were out in the yard, you didn't see Stan?"

"No. But then it would be unlikely that I would."

Joe was at once puzzled. "How come?"

"Blind spots." Kane stood and moved to the windows, gesturing for Joe and Amy to follow. "We have most of the yard covered by CCTV, but there are areas which are not, and some of those areas are practically invisible even when you're in the yard. One of them is the workshops and the area outside them, the maintenance yard."

Kane pointed over to the far left, where a young man dressed in mechanic's overalls, emerged from a low building carrying what looked to Joe like a bent and twisted bumper bar, which he threw in a skip full of similar scrap parts.

Large, concertina doors were open, but because of the strong sunlight, Joe could see almost nothing of the building's interior. By concentrating, he could eventually make out the front of the STAC bus.

"The workshops are set back from the main yard," Kane was saying, "and they're on a lower level. As you enter the site, unless you looked into that corner, you wouldn't see them. At this end of the yard, you can't see them because they're blocked off by vehicles on the tractor and trailer parks."

"And you don't even have CCTV coverage of that area?"

"It's not considered a risk," Kane explained. "The mechanics don't have access to the Sort Centre or any of the storage warehouses, so it's impossible for them to steal anything. In fact, Joe, this office and the top of the stairs on this floor are the only two places where the workshops can be seen. Stand anywhere else on site, and they're invisible... well, you can see the roof of the building, but that's all."

Joe brought his gaze closer to them, staring straight down onto the trailer parks. Lined up three deep, he found it easy to correlate the view he had had the day before from close up.

He gestured down at the trailers. "And I take it that the individual trailer parks are not covered by CCTV either?"

"You couldn't do that without putting up a camera every three metres," Amy said, "but there are cameras at either end of the building which cover the roadway in front of the trailers." She, too, pointed down at the broad road between building and parks where a shunt tug was moving slowly along as if the driver was looking for a particular trailer.

At the very back of the parks, barely visible beyond the top of the rear trailer, was a tarmac car park half filled with private vehicles. Joe recalled seeing a wire mesh fence behind the trailers but he could not see it from this angle.

He turned from the window and leaned on the narrow, metal sill facing both. "Now there's a thing. Dave, did you say to me that the only route into and out of this building was through the security scanner at the main entrance?"

Kane nodded. "What about it?"

"And Amy, did you say that Stan was clearing out his locker and then he was on his way home?"

She, too, nodded. "Yes."

"So what was he doing here?" Joe aimed his finger down at the trailer lines. "See, when Keith and I first arrived yesterday, we were told to stick to the pedestrian footpath while we were wandering round the yard. I noticed that all your car parks are over there." He pointed to the blank, west wall of the office. "When I followed you out through the Dispatch exit, Dave, I also noticed that there's only a narrow footpath outside Dispatch, which runs parallel to the building, and takes drivers to their tractors, also parked over there." Again, he indicated the west yard. "But even if you did have a footpath running along or between the trailers, which would be bloody daft, it still doesn't account for why Stan was there and not on his way off site."

They exchanged resigned glances, and Kane sighed. "He was sneaking out using a short cut."

"A short cut?"

Amy faced the windows and pointed to the small car park Joe had spotted behind the trailers. "That is the official driver's car park. Every department is allocated a parking area for its staff. It's not a rule that's strictly enforced, especially in the autumn when we're in the run up to Christmas and we have a lot of temp labour on site, but technically, that is where the drivers are supposed to park their cars, and most of them do. Now, behind the trailers is a mesh fence."

"I saw it yesterday," Joe told her. "When we found Stan."

"What you won't have noticed is that behind the trailer at the back of park fifteen is a hole in that wire mesh where someone has cut it away from the metal pillar. Sometimes, if Dispatch is busy and no one is taking particular notice, drivers will sneak out through the Dispatch exit, and duck down park fifteen, where they can't be seen by anyone other than a passing shunter or driver, and nip through the fence to their cars."

"And is it a problem?" Joe asked.

"A hell of a problem," Kane admitted. "They're evading a potential search, which is a breach of company rules. It's a disciplinary offence."

Joe frowned. "Then why hasn't the hole been stitched up?"

"Budget," Kane replied. "We reported it to General Maintenance in January, but they were short of money. They got their new budget at the beginning of this month, and it's on the schedule for repair."

"Not that it will last long," Amy said. "One of the drivers will only cut through it again."

Joe was still puzzled. "But why do they do it?"

"Time," Amy explained. "You see, Joe, at the end of a shift, the drivers sign off in Dispatch, about a hundred yards from their cars. From there, they have to walk through the Sort Centre, go through the scanner, where they could be pulled for a search, then they have to leave the building and walk all the way round the site to their cars. On a bad night, finishing at the same time as the Sort Centre staff, say, the queue at the scanner is usually at its longest, and it can take anything up to twenty minutes to get from Dispatch to your car. By cutting through the hole in the fence, they're in the car in less than two minutes and no hassle."

Joe absorbed the information. "And Stan made regular use of this short cut, did he?"

Amy shrugged. "No more than anyone else, I don't think. He wouldn't go that way every night. Maybe once a week, once a fortnight. And he probably went that way yesterday as a way of thumbing his nose at the company."

Joe's versatile mind began to follow fresh tracks, piecing together the events into various scenarios, and after a moment's deep thought, one of them became more likely than any other.

"Stan was killed in the middle of the trailers on park fifteen. But how many people knew he would go that way? Huh? How many people knew he would leave the site via that route? No one. He made a decision on the spur of the moment, and that means the confrontation was also a spur of the moment thing." Joe picked up his notes and scanned them. "Peter could have seen him from here and hurried after him."

Amy shook her head. "Stan would have been on the car park by the time Peter got downstairs and out into the yard through Dispatch."

"True," Joe agreed. "But he could have called Stan back, couldn't he? And you said Stan was in a blazing mood, so he wouldn't have hesitated to come back and face Peter."

Amy let out a sigh of utter frustration. "For the last time, Joe, it was not Peter. I told you, any fight between these two would have been no worse than handbags."

"Then give me some other leads, Amy." Joe returned to the table, tore off a fresh sheet of notepaper and consulting his notes began to scribble. When he was through, he invited them both to lean over his shoulder to see what he had written.

Stan arr	11:10
Arrested	11:40
Ret wth Amy	13:15
Mtg open	13:30
Mtg end	13:50
Kane to tractor	14:10
Amy to office	14:10
Kane ret	14:40
Kane sees Peter	14:50
Peter arr security	15:05
Stan found	15:30

"Now look here. Stan left the building at about quarter past two. Both you and Dave were gone by ten past. Peter was seen at ten past, and again at ten to three. Stan must have been killed in that forty minute gap. You had time to do it, Amy, and at pinch, Dave, you could have done too, but favourite is still Peter. Burrows will leap on this, but I'm with you. I don't believe it was Peter. He had the opportunity, yes, he probably had the motive, but you, Dave, said he was back in this office when you returned at ten to three. Did he look injured?

"No. I told you. He was quiet, but he didn't look as if he was in any pain."

"And yet, between you seeing him at ten to three and him arriving at security at five past, the blow which he'd received overtook him and killed him. And he must have spent a good deal of that fifteen minute gap making his way from here to security. It also means that although he was in terrible pain after the fight with Stan, made his way back up to this floor first." Joe shook his head. "No, I don't think it was Peter, but who else? Amy you had the motive and opportunity. Dave, you had the opportunity, but do you have a motive?"

"No, I don't, and Amy, in case you've forgotten, has an alibi."

"There are plenty of other men – and women – in this place who would have cheerfully throttled Stan," Amy said. "Megan in Dispatch, for instance. She was Terry Dodd's girlfriend for long enough, but Stan split them up a few years ago."

"Alf Sclater's another," Kane said. "He caught his daughter at it with Stan in the gent's lavatories here. Stan was suspended, and Alf's daughter only just managed to save her job."

"He was a bit of a ladies' man, then?" Joe said, trying to suppress a note of envy in his voice.

"You shouldn't be envy him, Joe," Amy advised. "He caused a lot of trouble for a lot of people, men and women alike, and I always wondered what he would do when he got older. Alone, no one to look after him."

"He never got the chance to grow older alone, did he?" Joe

pointed out. Dragging them back on topic, he said, "Right, so we have plenty of bodies who might be in the frame for killing Stan, but why Peter?"

The pair exchanged blank stares and Joe ran through his notes again.

"I'm sorry, Joe, I don't understand," Amy protested.

"Another pal of mine, a teacher, once told me that if people can't answer your questions it's because you're asking the wrong ones. I'm obviously asking it wrong. What I'm saying is, if Peter and Stan did not kill each other, we can find plenty of motives for having a go at Stan, but why have a go at Peter? Why kill him? There's nothing obvious and Burrows will see that as another indication that it was a straight fight between the two men."

"So where do we go from there?" Kane asked.

Joe shrugged and sank into his thoughts. He was beginning to wish he had never accepted the challenge, but even as the thought crossed his mind, he knew he could never have resisted it. It was exactly the kind of puzzle he enjoyed the most. He also knew that even if Burrows' theory was the only one that made any kind of sense, it was wrong. Peter Cruikshank and Stan Crowther had not killed each other. But how could he prove...

"Did you say you had CCTV at either end of the building?" he asked.

Again, Kane nodded. "All four corners as a matter of fact. Round here, they look along this side of the building and around the corners into the east and west yards."

"So if Stan really did go out that way, and if Peter followed him, the CCTV would have caught them as they came out of the Dispatch exit?"

"I never thought of that," Amy confessed, "but yes, it probably did."

Obviously worried, Kane chewed his lip. "It could take days to get hold of the footage though."

"Hang on, Dave, I thought you ran this place."

"I run the transport department, Joe. But security are not employed by Ballantynes. It's a failsafe. Everyone here, from the Chief Executive down to the lavatory cleaner, is liable for search when they leave the building. The only way you can ensure that no one pulls strings to avoid that search is to keep security separate: autonomous. The CCTV footage is theirs, not ours, and in order to view it we have to put in a written request. On average it takes three days for the footage to reach us."

Joe snorted, stood up and gathered his belongings. "And you think that'll stop Burrows? It won't stop me, either. Take me to the man in charge. I'll show you how to get it now."

"Actually, it's a woman."

Chapter Nine

When they entered The Exchequer at a few minutes past noon, neither Sheila nor Brenda were surprised to find an irritated Vaughan waiting for them.

Without being invited, he joined them, fiddling with a glass of lager, and had no hesitation answering when they asked how he had tracked them down. "If I hadn't found you here, I'd have come over to the Monarch at some time during the day."

"It's so nice to feel wanted, isn't it, Sheila?" Brenda knocked back a generous slug of Campari.

"I reserved a table for four last night, and you never showed up."

"By the time he returned to the hotel last night, Joe was very tired," Sheila said. "He couldn't be bothered going out for dinner. We suggested he ring you and let you know, but once he found out who you were, he got quite angry."

"Well, that's only to be understood, but—"

"He also told us to avoid you like the plague," Brenda cut in.

"I understand how Murray feels, but you're only hearing—"

This time it was Sheila who interrupted. "I notice he's suddenly become Murray, rather than Joe, or the more polite *Mister* Murray. Quite adversarial."

"I am trying to build business premises which will improve Sanford." A note of exasperation had crept into Vaughan's voice. "*Mister* Murray doesn't appear to understand that. And that's why I followed him all the way to Blackpool. To try and get the message across."

"The message being, you're putting Joe out of business … or trying to."

Vaughan countered Brenda's candour with a glower. "You've only heard his side of the story, Mrs Jump. He has been offered alternative premises."

"On the industrial estate the other side of the road," Brenda said, "where he will lose the larger part of his trade."

"He was offered generous compensation."

"And what about us?" Sheila demanded. "Joe is a good friend, and an excellent employer, but he's no fool when it comes to business. He's been in the trade all his life. If he accepts your offer, he will have no choice but to dispense with one of us. But you don't care about such things, do you, Mr Vaughan? And all this nonsense of Sanford's welfare is precisely that; nonsense. All you really care about is the return on your investment, and The Lazy Luncheonette stands in the way of that, doesn't it?"

"That is not true. My project, the redevelopment of Britannia Parade, will create jobs. Proper jobs. Not part time, temporary vacancies in retail, but long-term, secure positions for professional people."

"As well as raking in huge rents for you and your company." Brenda smiled mock-sweetly. "No sale."

"Ladies, ladies, please…" Vaughan trailed off, and looked to one side, then the other. It was as if he was checking that no one was listening in, but both women guessed he was formulating his words, calculating his approach and weighing the likely responses. "Let me make a personal offer to each of you. I know how bad it can be when you lose your job at your age—"

"At our age?" Sheila was disgusted. "We're not yet ready for the nursing home, you know."

"Or the knackers yard."

"Brenda. Must you?"

"It's what they were called, Sheila—"

"What is wrong with you people?" Vaughan interrupted. "Why are you so set against progress?"

"Because we don't consider your shiny office blocks to be progress," Sheila told him. "If they were decent, affordable homes, then maybe."

"If they were decent, affordable industrial premises which would employ ordinary people, perhaps," Brenda said. "But your development will put us out of work and do nothing to tackle general unemployment in the town. I'm willing to bet that most of the lawyers, accountants and architects who move in won't even live in Sanford."

"Ten thousand… Each."

Vaughan's sudden declaration silenced both women.

"All you have to do is persuade Murray to get out. And I'll make sure it's tax free."

He was greeted by silence once more.

He relaxed, obviously feeling he was in complete control of the situation. "Come on, what do you say? Ten grand each. Murray – or the government – will pay you severance and then you'll be just free and well off."

"It's a tempting offer, Mr Vaughan," Sheila said. "Don't you think, Brenda?"

"Very tempting. But can we trust you to deliver."

"I'll have half of it for you tomorrow, or even later this afternoon."

They exchanged superior glances and smiles, then stood, ready to leave.

"No pressure, Mr Vaughan," Sheila said. "Brenda will answer for us both."

With a sweeping gesture, Brenda threw her left hand out and knocked Vaughan's glass over. The beer spilled across the table and splashed onto his light-coloured, casual trousers. With a cry, he shot backwards, but not fast enough to prevent his lap taking most of the spilled beer.

"Oh, I am sorry. Here. Let me pay for another one." Taking a two pound coin from her purse, Brenda tossed it on the table. "You know where you can stick your money, Mr Vaughan, and if you hassle us again, it won't be spilled beer on your trousers. I'll take a scalpel to you and your wife will need a lover."

***

As Kane had forecast, Sandra Hamilton refused point blank when they confronted her in reception. With Reg standing by, assuming the role of supporter according to Joe's best guess, she shook her head the moment Kane asked.

"I'm sorry, Mr Kane, but you know the rules. That footage doesn't belong to Ballantynes. It's ours, and you must put in a written request if you want to see it."

A small, mousey-haired woman in her mid-forties, she was still reading her hair care magazine when they arrived in reception, and Joe mentally questioned the wisdom of the security company in appointing her as shift manager. He recalled her bursting into tears when Peter Cruikshank died the previous day, and it seemed to him that someone so emotional and so disinterested should not even be in security work, never mind running the show.

When, however, Dave Kane asked for the tapes, the change in her was startling. The apparently vacuous, disinterested passenger was gone, replaced by a sharp-eyed, sharp-tongued supervisor not willing to stand any argument.

"Please, Sandra, it's vital that we look at those images. We need—"

"No, Mr Kane. You know the rules. I am not allowed to let anyone see those images without written authority."

Joe shouldered his way to the counter. "Excuse me, but—"

She cut him off far more rudely than she had Kane. "You have no authority here, so kindly mind your own business."

Joe buried the flash of anger which tempted him to bite her head off, and confined his response to simple logic. "Wrong. I've been authorised by Ballantynes to investigate this business."

Sandra glowered back at him. "Irrelevant. I've already said, I

108

don't work for Ballantynes and by agreement the security footage is not their property. The answer is no."

"It's vital that we see them, Sandra," Kane urged. "The written request will follow."

"I'm sorry, Mr Kane, but I said no, and I mean no. Stick to procedures."

"Will you say the same to Chief Inspector Burrows?" Joe asked.

Again she glared at him, her tiny eyes pinpoints of anger. "He asked, I told him the same thing. He needs a warrant."

"Wrong," Joe declared. "Police and Criminal Evidence Act, 1984. In the course of investigating a major crime, where the police officer suspects that evidence pertaining to that crime is withheld, he may demand it without the need for a search warrant, and if the suspect continues to withhold the evidence, the suspect may be arrested for obstructing a police officer in the course of his duties."

Sandra blanched. "What?"

"This is a murder investigation, woman. If he suspects this footage can point to the killer, Burrows doesn't need a search warrant, and if you continue to refuse, he can arrest and charge you for obstruction." Joe dug not his ubiquitous gilet and retrieved his phone. "Right now, of course, Burrows doesn't know that yesterday's footage may show him the killer. We've only just realised it ourselves. But he will in a few minutes."

"I'm just doing my job," Sandra whined.

"Not for much longer," Joe assured her as he called up Sheila's number. "Or am I wrong in thinking that a security officer with a criminal record can no longer hold a licence. And obstructing the police is a criminal matter."

Her features turned pale. "You mean I could be fired for it?"

Joe nodded. "Eventually."

"But I could be fired for giving you access to the footage, too."

"Not if we explain," Kane said. "You may not work for

Ballantynes, but your co-operation will be noted and your employer will more than likely reward you for it."

"Want me to call Burrows?" Joe asked.

She vacillated while Reg stood by looking helpless. At length Joe pushed the connect button and put the phone to his ear.

"All right," Sandra said. "Tell me what you need."

"Hello, Joe," Sheila's voice rang in his ear.

"Sorry. Dialled the wrong number." Joe cut the connection and smiled at Sandra. "That's more like it. We need to see footage from the south side of the building between ten past two and, say, ten to three yesterday afternoon. We can fast forward through it. If you're not happy about that, we're happy to let you review it."

Sandra made notes. "What are you looking for?"

"Peter Cruikshank and Stan Crowther leaving the building by the Dispatch exit."

"I'll get onto it."

Sandra hurried over to her console while Amy, Kane and Joe stepped back from the counter.

"Police and Criminal Evidence Act," Kane muttered. "Congratulations, Joe."

He smiled back and kept his voice low. "I thought it was good, too. Off the cuff like that. Course, it's rubbish." The other two were surprised. "I have a niece who's a copper, so I've heard of PACE, but I wouldn't know one end of the act from the other."

Amy giggled and Kane laughed aloud.

Their humour was cut short by Reg, leaning on the counter as he spoke to them. "Excuse me, Mr Murray, Mr Kane, Ms Willows, but I can tell you that Stan Crowther didn't leave by the Dispatch exit."

Joe's head turned so fast, he almost wrenched his neck. "What?"

"I signed him out yesterday afternoon, a few minutes before you and your driver turned up, Mr Murray. He left through this door." Reg pointed to the outside world.

"Do the police know this?" Joe demanded.

"Shouldn't think so. They didn't ask. When they spoke to us yesterday, it was all about Mr Cruikshank."

From the back of the work area, Sandra called out, "Still want me to look?"

"Yes," Joe insisted. "But instead of looking for Crowther, just look for Cruikshank. We need to know if he stepped out into the yard through the Dispatch exit, and if he did, we need to know where he went." He turned his attention to Reg. "You're sure about Crowther leaving this way?"

"Definite. Odd situation, to be honest. He insisted on a search."

"Come again?"

"Well, he came through the scanner, it didn't trigger," Reg explained. "Normally, I would have let him go, and normally, the driver would be happy about that, but he insisted on a pat-down search and a check of his bag."

"You found nothing untoward?" Kane asked.

"Clean and green," Reg confirmed.

Joe raised his eyebrows at Kane and Amy, and the union woman replied.

"He'd just been suspended. My guess is he wanted to be certain the company couldn't bring anything else against him, so he left via the official route and had Reg confirm that he was not taking anything with him that he shouldn't have."

"Sounds sensible enough, but the big question now is, how did he end up on park fifteen?" Joe scribbled out his mobile number and handed it to Reg. "When Sandra is finished, ask her to bell me with the result." He turned back to the manager and union woman. "Can we retrace the route he would have taken to his car?"

"No problem," Kane said, "but to what end?"

"I don't know," Joe admitted. "Sometimes it helps to, er, reconstruct a victim's last minutes. The cops do it all the time."

"Yes but that's usually to help witness recall, Joe," Amy pointed out.

"Well, in this case it's to help me clear some of the clutter from my head." Joe beamed a persuasive smile on her and was rewarded by a similar smile of genuine warmth from her.

***

Lying half prone on the bed in his room at the Hilton, Vaughan cursed down the telephone and kicked his briefcase further down the mattress. "I want this matter dealt with, Queenan," he hissed. "I want that damned café levelled. I am sick of the delays, I am sick of the excuses and I am triple sick of Joe bloody Murray and his staff."

"Calm yourself, Gerard," Queenan said. "There are procedures which must be observed. The CPO has been issued, Murray has appealed. We have to let the law take its course."

"And how many more times do I have to tell you that every day is costing me hundreds of pounds." Vaughan glowered at his stained trousers, thrown over an armchair. "And his girlfriends have just put up my laundry bill."

"What?"

"Never mind. Now what the hell are you doing about Murray?"

"I told you. There is nothing we can do. But don't worry, Gerard. He won't win. These appeals never come to anything, and Murray's is based on the thinnest of pretexts."

"You're not listening, Queenan. I want him out, I want that building down, I want my people working and I do not want to hang around for some legal committee to make up its mind. Either get him out of there or I will."

He cut the connection and stared at the featureless walls of his room. Then, in a paroxysm of blind rage, he threw the mobile at the wall.

The pique of fury evaporated as quickly as it had boiled up, and he instantly regretted the broken phone. Stretching across the bed, he yanked his briefcase closer, flipped open the lid and took out a smartphone. With barely a glance at the menus, he called up the number and dialled.

"Appleby? I want you and your pal here five minutes ago."

***

Joe, Kane and Amy followed the marked pedestrian path away from the building and towards the main gates. From here, the trailer parks in question were invisible on the north side of the building, and looking at the layout, Joe guessed that the closest of those parks would not become visible until they were past the gatehouse and walking down the west side of the site.

But the loading bays on the west side were all full and there was a wide roadway between them and the staff car parks.

"Could Crowther have taken a short cut through the actual yard to get to park fifteen?" Joe asked, waving his hand at the roadway.

"He could and it's doubtful whether any of the shunters would have challenged him," Kane replied. "They're used to seeing drivers milling about the yard, and at that time, it wasn't generally known that Stan had been suspended."

"It doesn't make much sense, though," Amy commented. "If he was going to take a short cut, why didn't he just go out the Dispatch door?"

"Logical," Joe agreed, "but people don't always behave logically. Stan was angry, he was probably still half drunk, too. He may have got out here and thought, 'Why am I going this way I'm all but fired, so why don't I break all the rules'. It could happen."

They reached the lower end of the yard, and from here Joe could make out the entrance to the workshop and its approach yard. Inside, now clearly visible despite the bright sunshine and darker interior, was the STAC bus in one of the repair bays.

"Our vehicle will be ready by Monday, Dave?"

"We'll be speaking to your driver, but as I understand it, the parts have arrived. They only need fitting and polishing up to match the rest of the vehicle."

"There was no structural damage?"

"Chassis and framework were checked, Joe, and they're fine."

They turned to the right and, following the path round the car park, entered parking area H. There were many private cars in it, reflecting the number of drivers working.

"On Easter Saturday, too." Joe's muttered comment was meant only for his ears. Aloud, he asked, "Why put the drivers so far away from the building and the exits?"

"Ergonomics," Amy replied. "Drivers work longer hours and irregular shifts. The Sort Centre runs a three-shift system. Transport runs only two. That means there's more movement of traffic with the cars belonging to the warehouse crew, so it's better to have them closer to the exit gate."

"I must say, you're pretty well organised."

"It's a massive operation, Joe. We have to think of everything."

Stood in the middle of the driver's car park, Joe looked around.

To the north and east, away from the building, was only the high perimeter wall. To the west the workshop yard had once more become invisible, but the building itself was prominent. To the south, however, all Joe could see were the rear of trailers and peeking just above them the top floor of the Sort Centre.

He pointed at the few windows breaking up the line of the building. "Your office?"

Kane nodded and pointed further along to four small, frosted-glass windows. "Third floor toilet and locker rooms." His finger swept across the building, past his office to the western end and a single panoramic window. "The staircase. I told you. This area can be seen only from there and my office."

Closer to them and at ground level, Joe looked along the

wire mesh fence which sealed off the yard from the car parks. Angle iron supports were set in concrete every five yards or so, and although it appeared intact, he could see where part of the mesh had been cut from a support.

"Which is park fifteen?"

Amy pointed it out the other side of the hole in the mesh, and the moment she did, Joe spotted the police crime scene tape attached to the nose of the rear trailer and back of the one in front.

"So, Stan is making his way here, and he ends up there." He pointed to the crime scene. "How? Why? You are sure his car was parked here?"

"It still is," Amy said, and moved across to a red Hyundai.

Joe followed, and circled the car. Nothing in it to attract any attention. And from the rear of the car, the crime scene could not be seen. He moved to the front, and as he passed, he noticed a black holdall on the passenger seat.

"His bag," he said. "Now I'm beginning to understand."

From the opposite side of the car, Kane pointed to the steering wheel. "The keys are in the ignition, too."

"That settles it, then." Joe hurried around the car and glanced again at park fifteen. "It's obvious what went on." He tutted. "If Burrows' people had checked the car yesterday, they would have known, too."

"If his keys were in the car, they won't have realised he owned one," Amy pointed out. Her matter-of-fact tone switched quickly to puzzlement. Puzzlement. "What went on, Joe?"

Rather than answer immediately, Joe searched through his pockets seeking a handkerchief or tissue and could not find one. With another irritated cluck, he asked, "Dave, can you get onto your mechanics and ask someone to bring me over a pair of those plastic gloves they use. The disposable ones."

Kane took out his phone. "No problem, but you're not thinking of opening the car, are you?"

"Yes. I want to check his bag."

"But the police—"

Joe cut him off with a broad grin. "Don't need to know, do they?"

While Kane rang the workshop, Joe explained his deductions to Amy. Waving at the hole in the fence, he said, "Stan obviously made it to his car, threw his bag on the passenger seat, and put the keys in the ignition. So why did he then go back through the fence? There's only one answer when you think about it. I still can't see the crime scene from here, so it means someone appeared behind park fifteen and called him over."

"His killer?"

Joe nodded. "Who else? That means it would have to be someone Stan knew, but I figure that's been the case all along. It also means Stan was not expecting an attack, or if he was, he'd be confident of dealing with it."

Amy huffed. "Peter. Again."

"Maybe, maybe not." Joe tried to put on a sympathetic face. "Amy, I know you find this hard to believe, and I do myself, but you have to accept that so far, the prime suspect is Peter."

Dropping his phone back into his pocket, Kane joined them in time to hear the declaration. "I don't believe it either. So what do you expect to find in Stan's car?"

"The flask?" Joe sounded more hopeful than positive.

With another delay in the offing, Joe wandered along park fifteen and spent a few moments looking down at the crime scene, but it told him nothing he did not know already. As he returned to the car park, his phone rang. It was an unrecognised number. He put the phone to his ear, announced himself and listened for a moment. Putting the phone away, he said to his two companions, "That was Sandra. Peter Cruikshank never left the building yesterday."

A mixture of relief and satisfaction crossed Amy's face. "So it wasn't him. I said it all along, didn't I?"

"It merely begs more questions, though," Joe said. "The major problem now is how did the killer know that Stan was leaving the building on his way home? I take it everyone in Dispatch would know?"

Amy nodded. "They were not told, but it would have been easy to put it all together."

"So do we need to look at your Dispatch staff?" Joe muttered.

He had meant it to be taken as a serious consideration, but Amy replied anyway. "There would be one or two candidates."

Joe would have responded, but he spotted a young man dressed in a boiler suit, making his way across to the car park towards them. "We can talk about that later. Peter's not completely out of it, but it's looking very unlikely." He nodded at the approaching individual. "Is this one of your mechanics, Dave?"

"Apprentice," Kane corrected.

The lad arrived and handed over a pair of protective gloves, Kane took a moment to thank him and then lectured him briefly on the dangers of playing games in the workshop area, and the young man left again.

"Sorry, Joe, but you have to keep ramming the message home."

"It's time you got CCTV in the workshop yard," Amy grumbled.

Joe ignored them, pulled the tight-fitting gloves on, and with his fingertips, opened the car door. He checked the key first, and found that it was simply slotted into the ignition. It had not been turned on. He leaned across and unzipped the bag. Looking inside, he found the same mess Amy had turned up the previous day. Satisfied, he zipped the bag shut again and climbed out of the car, closing the door behind him.

"That settles it for me. Stan's flask is not in the bag."

"But we knew that, Joe."

"No you didn't," Joe corrected Kane. "You knew it wasn't

117

there when he was in your office with you, Peter and Amy. But Amy left him alone to clear out his locker. He could have hidden it in there and taken it out again before leaving the building. But whatever happened to it, it was not with Stan, and for my money, that means whoever killed him took it earlier in the day."

Chapter Ten

"You demanded that I keep you up to date," Joe said testily. "That's just what I'm doing. Peter Cruikshank never left the building. Stan Crowther did, but he walked all the way round the yard to his car where he put the keys in the ignition and dropped his bag off, before coming back to park fifteen where he was murdered."

After a call from Joe, Burrows and his team had joined them on the car park. The forensic team went to work on Crowther's car and he responded to Joe's argument.

"You're giving me theory, Murray, not fact."

"There are facts, and the theory was built to fit around them. I repeat, Peter Cruikshank never left the building. So he did not kill Crowther."

"They could have fought inside," Burrows argued. "We know that Cruikshank didn't die immediately."

"We also know that he made his way from his office to security before he collapsed. And that was after only the single blow. You're telling us that Crowther, who had been hit twice, managed to get from that same office, or at least the third floor, all the way through security, where he insisted on a search, then right the way to his car before deciding that he would walk up park fifteen and drop dead."

Ignoring most of Joe's argument, Burrows said, "That could be the very reason he was walking up park fifteen. He was fading fast and he went for help."

Joe tossed this over in his head, and found that it had a ring of possibility about it. But he was not about to say so to Burrows. "You still haven't told us how he managed to get all this way before he finally dropped."

"I'll know more about that when I get the post mortem results."

"Then speculate."

"I don't like—"

"All right, I will. My guess is that both men died as a result of either skull fracture or cervical spine fracture. Death needn't be instantaneous, but would leave both disoriented, just as we noticed with Peter. Stan had been struck twice. His death might not have been instantaneous either, but the second blow probably delivered while he was floored by the first, would have knocked him out. He wouldn't have come round. He died while he was unconscious. We know that he was lucid enough to demand a search when he passed through the security scanner. That means he was killed where he was found. We know that Peter never left the building, and that being the case there is no way he and Stan did this to each other. You're looking for someone else, as I predicted all along."

"We'll have to see, won't we?" With that, Burrows marched off to join his team.

"He's determined to pin it on Peter and Stan, isn't he?" Amy asked.

Joe shrugged. "No, I don't think so. He probably just doesn't like his thunder being stolen. He may have already decided that I'm right, but he's not gonna say so."

They stood watching in silence as the forensic people worked systematically on the car and the bag, taking items, cataloguing them and bagging them up.

Joe leaned against the wire mesh fence and basked in the glorious afternoon sunshine. He wondered idly where Sheila and Brenda were, and whether it was time to cut out and rejoin them. He decided that they would probably be shopping and since he disliked shopping, he was better off where he was.

"What do we do now, Joe?"

Kane's query brought Joe from his reverie. "What? Oh, sorry.

Yeah. I reckon we need to think about that flask."

"And what will that prove? Other than Stan was drunk, which we already know."

"Yeah, and that's what doesn't make much sense. Y'see, if Stan added booze to his own flask I can see him hiding it from you lot, but I don't know why since it was his claim that it had been doctored. He would have been happy to have you analyse it. On the other hand, if Peter really had doctored the flask, I can understand him hiding it, too. But how did he get hold of it? Why did Stan not take it with him when he left the building? Where the hell is it? There are just too many unanswered questions about this missing flask. They may mean something, they may not, but we won't know until we find it."

Kane waved an arm at the vast site. "Do you know how many skips, compactors and general refuse bins we have, Joe? We passed at least three on the way from reception. If Stan really did throw it away, it could be in any of them."

"Or Peter, come to that," Amy said. "He could have got it earlier in the day, couldn't he? You know. When Stan first got back. There was a long time between Stan turning up at the main gate, and the four of us meeting in your office, Dave."

"Now you're sounding like Burrows," Joe said with a grin directed at the chief inspector, who was now listening on his mobile phone.

"When I say Peter, I mean it could apply to just about anyone," Amy corrected herself.

"Anyone who wanted to get Stan into trouble," Joe said, "and by all accounts that's most of Blackpool."

He fell silent as Burrows terminated his call and strode across to them.

"All right, Murray, you win. Both men suffered severe trauma to the cervical spine. The second blow probably killed Crowther. Cruikshank would have been dazed and probably partly paralysed, and as we know, he made it to reception. It means that Crowther died where he was found, and since

Cruikshank never left the building – according to you – he cannot have killed Crowther and vice versa."

Reminding himself that two men had died, Joe suppressed a feeling of satisfaction at the news, but went on to correct Burrows on a minor point. "It's not according to me. It's Sandra, the head of security. She checked the CCTV footage for the relevant time and she says Cruikshank never stepped out of the building."

"How did you get to see that?" Burrows demanded. "She insisted we get a warrant."

Joe grinned. "I used my natural charm on her. You should try it sometime."

"Bog off. Mind, I do think it's time I was looking at this CCTV stuff. This case is now a full-blown double murder investigation."

***

Joe's guess on the whereabouts of Sheila and Brenda was slightly off the mark. They had been shopping, but by two o'clock, after a walk round the crowded and narrow aisles of Bonny Street Market, they were in the Waterloo Inn, just off the promenade near Central Pier, where they had met up with George Robson, Owen Frickley, Les Tanner and Sylvia Goodson, and Alec and Julia Staines.

"Where's Joe?" George asked. "Still out there, playing Miss Marple?"

"As far as we know, yes," Sheila replied. "And we could have done with him today."

"How come?"

Brenda waved at their bags of purchases. "Pack mule."

George laughed. "I always knew he was good for more than steak and kidney pies."

Brenda glanced at the door where Vaughan and two taller, stockier men had just entered. "Joe's usually good at sorting out problems, too." She indicated the property man with a slow nod of the head. "Problems like him."

George looked them over and sneered. "Easy peasy. You don't need to worry while I'm here, Brenda."

"The day I have to rely on you, George Robson, is the day I hand in me cards." She rounded on Vaughan. "Can't you take a hint?"

He indicated the men either side of him. "Meet Mr Appleby and his associate, Mr McNeill. They are here, Mrs Jump, to ensure I don't take another unexpected shower. Where's Murray?"

"He's not here," Sheila replied. "Now why don't you leave us alone, Mr Vaughan?"

"Did I not just say I wanted to speak to the butcher, not the block?"

"Go away," Brenda ordered, "and take your tame gorillas with you. You're not impressing anyone."

"I will go when I have seen Murray, and not until. Now kindly step out of my way."

He made to move her aside with his arm, but George stepped between them.

"Keep your hands to yourself, pal."

Vaughan looked down his nose at George. "Mind your own business, you fat idiot."

"Watch it—"

There was a dangerous edge to George's voice, cut off when Vaughan interrupted and began stressing his words with repeated pokes in the chest. "I told you to mind your own business, you moron. Or don't you understand plain English? Do I have to ask my colleagues to teach you what that means?"

George's face coloured. He drew back his fist.

"George, no," Brenda cried.

George's fist flew forward.

***

"I still don't understand why Stan's thermos is so important," Amy said.

They were seated in the deserted drivers' rest room, alongside Dispatch.

"Not all our drivers work weekends," Kane had explained, "and those who are working don't spend time in here. They have work out there." He waved at the walls to indicate the outside world.

Kane had moved to the drinks machine, and Joe had sunk into depressed thoughts. Although pleased that his early deductions had been accepted, he was no nearer identifying a suspect, let alone solving the case. Amy's question stirred his thoughts, but those same mental gymnastics produced only more of the same questions.

Accepting a cup of coffee from Kane, he sipped and grimaced at the bitter taste. "Worse than The Lazy Luncheonette." Putting the cup down, he cleared his throat, he finally answered Amy's question. "The events are linked. Or do we imagine that it's all coincidence?"

"But I don't see how they're linked."

"We've demonstrated that Stan was murdered by an as yet unknown, third party. That third party must also have spiked his flask. Let's not worry about the how or when for the moment. Let's just accept that he did. Was he trying to get Stan fired or hoping he would end up so drunk that he would injure, even kill himself on the road? Let's imagine that had happened. What would the police have done? Gone through the truck, found the flask, tested it, and then pointed the finger straight at Stan. Drunk driving. But it didn't happen. Instead, Stan managed to get his rig back here with only a few minor scrapes and that put the killer in a difficult position. That flask was evidence. Stan was a witness, even if he was blathered."

"So he had to do away with both Stan and the flask," Kane said.

"Correct. Murder is a lot riskier than spiking a flask, but he knew how it can be done. If we can recover the flask, we may get some evidence as to the killer's identity, if only from the booze he used." Joe frowned and finally admitted what he had known for some time. "I'm sorry, Dave, but I'm just about at the end of my reach. There are too many suspects and you'll need the police and their scientific services to narrow down the possibles."

A flash of disappointment crossed Kane's portly features. It was only fleeting, but to Joe it was unmistakable.

"Too many suspects?"

"Hundreds," Joe said with a nod.

Amy was as puzzled as Kane. "I don't see where you get that from, Joe."

"Think about it. I just said that whoever tampered with the flask is probably the killer. Now, who had the opportunity? You two, Peter and everyone in Dispatch." Joe gestured through the windows to the office next door. "But it doesn't end there. While I was in here yesterday, waiting to speak to the police, I noticed bodies coming in from the Sort Centre to grab a cup of coffee or filling their bottles at the water cooler." He waved across the room at the machine. "Let's assume Stan went off to the toilet or somewhere and left his bag and the flask here on the table. Someone comes in from the Sort Centre, spots the opportunity and takes it. Later, when Stan is away at the police station, our killer sees him being escorted through the Sort Centre and whips in here to take the flask out of the bag, then gets rid of it." He shook his head sadly, an admission of defeat. No. There are too many suspects for a one-man band like me." Frustration welled up and he threw the half empty cup into the waste bin.

"The police could take months," Kane complained.

"It happens." Joe wished he was still a smoker. At times like this, he would take out his tobacco tin and roll a cigarette, an act which he insisted had always helped clear his thoughts.

Pushing thoughts of cigarettes to the back of his mind, he

said, "You know, it's Peter's death I can't understand. I believe Stan was the target, but why was Peter killed? Did he know something or was he murdered to give us a red herring, a garden path we could be led along."

Amy shuddered visibly. "That's a pretty shoddy reason for killing someone."

"As far as I'm concerned, there is never a good reason for taking a life, but people do." Joe tutted irritably. "Stan's attacker had killed once, and he may not have thought twice about killing a second time to cover his tracks."

"In that case," Kane said, "you can't really know who was the target. The business with Stan may just have been designed to cover up Peter's murder."

Joe shook his head. "It's possible, but I don't think so. Stan was struck twice, remember. Making sure he was dead. Peter took only one blow. If he were the target, the killer would have made sure by hitting him a second time. I imagine the police have checked through Peter's desk?" When the manager nodded, Joe went on, "Pity. I thought there might have been a clue as to who attacked him."

"They did, too." Kane emptied his cup and threw it into the waste bin. "Aside from his phone, I don't think they found anything. Even that was on the desk, not in the drawers."

"How about his locker?" Amy asked. "Nothing in there?"

A slow look of surprise came to Kane's eyes. "They never checked his locker. They can't have done."

"Why?" Joe asked.

"Because they didn't know he had one. I forgot about it until Amy just mentioned it. If the police had asked, I'd have had to call security to come up with the key."

"Get onto security now," Joe ordered. "Ask them to get here with the key."

"It's not here. It's on the third floor."

Joe stood up. "Then tell them to meet us there."

***

The locker room was adjacent to the gents' toilets just along from Kane's office. Like that on the ground floor, there was a block of small lockers off to one side, opposite the high, narrow, frosted windows.

Having insisted on Kane signing the relevant authorisation, and had it witnessed by Amy, Terry Dodd turned his master key in locker 1459, threw open the door and stood back.

Amy stared in, eyes wide, and gasped. Kane, too, was astonished. Intrigued by their reaction, Joe looked in and amongst the trivia — a baseball cap, a pair of safety gloves, and a spare hi-vis vest — was a shiny, metal thermos.

"It's Stan's," Amy said and reached in to pick it up.

"Don't touch it," Joe ordered and pulled on the borrowed mechanic's gloves. "How do you know it's Stan's?"

"I can see his initials."

Using only his fingertips on the very base of the flask, Joe turned it until he could see the letters 'SC' scratched into the metal beneath the cup.

"We need Burrows and his people up here," he said, backing away from the locker and taking out his phone. He dialled the chief inspector, spent a moment or two explaining the situation and then dropping the phone back into his pocket, pushed the locker door to. "He's on his way. He's asked that we touch nothing but we all wait here, including you, Terry."

Dodd inclined his head. "Whatever."

"This looks like an attempt to frame Peter," Joe declared, moving away from the lockers and stripping off the gloves. "Terry, you're round and about quite a lot, how well did you know Peter Cruikshank?"

The big man shrugged. "As well as I know anyone else. We're a separate company, see. A contract company. We don't hobnob with the Ballantyne employees."

Joe's eyebrows rose. "Really? I'm told you had a thing with

one of the women in Dispatch."

Dodd's piggy eyes narrowed. "Megan. Yeah, but that was a few years back. And it was Stan Crowther who bubbled us, wasn't it? Got me hauled over the coals."

"Because he fancied her himself."

Dodd shrugged. "So they reckon."

Joe tossed the news around his agile mind. "You don't mind me saying but this is all a bit draconian, isn't it? I mean, it's not like you're working for the secret service or anything."

The security man gave this some thought. "That's true, and technically, there was nothing the company could do about me and Megan, but they could have moved me to another site. I prefer it here, so I called it a draw with Meg."

"The job was more important, huh?"

"That's right. You might not see it like that, but it's the way I chose."

"No, no. We're all entitled to make the decisions we … listen, Terry, you came into the Sort Centre yesterday. Did you see anything of Peter Cruikshank? Were you on this floor? Did you see anyone following him, or watching him or—"

"I came in for my afternoon break," Dodd cut in. "I was on the ground floor in the nearest rest room. I didn't see anything of him."

Joe felt his frustration rising again. "Yeah. Right. No worries."

Burrows entered, followed by two forensic officers. Putting on gloves, the chief inspector opened the locker, took out the thermos and removed the cup and the stopper. He sniffed at it and screwed up his face in disgust. He held it out for Joe, who also took a sniff.

There were a few dregs in the bottom of the glass interior and the odour was one of stewed coffee, mixed with aniseed.

"Absinthe?" Joe asked.

"Probably. Could be Pernod, but according to reports, Crowther was in a hell of a state when our people breathalysed him, so we're talking really potent spirits, and absinthe is favourite." He handed it to the nearest forensic man. "Dust for prints, get the bit that's left in there analysed."

The forensic officer bagged up the flask while his colleague began cataloguing and bagging the few items left in the locker.

"Throws it all up in the air again, don't you think? It looks like it was Cruikshank after all."

"No," Joe replied. "I think it was an attempt to frame Peter for getting Crowther drunk. I also think it may be the reason Peter was murdered, and five'll get you ten you find no prints on the thermos."

"All quite possible," Burrows conceded. "But it may also mean there was some further friction between the two men. Particularly if Cruikshank did spike the flask. I'll let you know."

"Oh, while we're here, there's a scuff mark with what looks like a hair attached to it on the landing at the top of the staircase. You might wanna get your boys to check it out."

Burrows nodded, and was about to say something when his mobile buzzed for attention. He took it from his pocket, checked the menu window and made the connection. "Chief Inspector Burrows."

He listened intently to the call, occasionally looking at Joe. His expression changed from amazement, to anger, back to surprise, then amazement and finally irritation as he thanked the caller and closed off the phone.

He concentrated on Joe. "Do you know a Mrs Sheila Riley and a Mrs Brenda Jump?"

"You know I do. They were at breakfast this morning."

"George Robson and Owen Frickley?"

"Two of my members. What's happened, Burrows?"

"How about Jeffrey Appleby and Gerard Vaughan?"

"I know Vaughan, I've never heard of Appleby. Come on, man, what is it?"

"There was an altercation at the Waterloo Arms about an hour ago. Our people went in and arrested four people who claim to be connected with the Sanford 3rd Age Club, along with Appleby, an associate of his named McNeil, and Vaughan. They're all at the station. When asked who they wanted to call, Mrs Riley said to contact you via me."

"I'd better get over there."

"It's on Bonny Street. You know where that is?"

"I'll find it."

"Let me run you down there, Joe," Amy offered.

***

"The Sanford 3rd Age Club?" the union woman asked as they pulled out of Ballantynes' main gate and turned left onto Squires Gate Lane, heading for the seafront.

"I'm chairman. My friends Sheila and Brenda are Secretary and Treasurer. We came up with the idea, oh, six, seven, years ago. Maybe longer. We have about three hundred members, all over fifty years of age, and we organise outings and events for the benefit of the members. This weekend is an official STAC outing."

"Stack?"

"S-T-A-C," Joe said. "It stands for—"

"Sanford 3rd Age Club," Amy cut in with a smile. "What a good idea."

"We think so. Most of our members are middle-aged rockers. Overage teddy boys and girls, reliving their past glories. The difference is these days they have plenty of cash and they know how to move plenty of booze. They're also hard and fast in their opinions and if you're smart, you don't pick an argument with the Sanford 3rd Age Club."

Amy turned right onto the seafront at Starr Gate and accelerated. Traffic was sparse, but as they neared the Pleasure Beach it began to pick up and their speed dropped as a consequence.

"And do they often get into fights in pubs?"

"Not usually," Joe replied. "Normally, it's verbal. I guess it's to do with Vaughan and his sidekicks."

She stopped at a set of lights outside the Pleasure Beach Casino and while Joe looked up at the complex latticework of rails and girders that formed The Big One, she asked, "And who is Vaughan?"

"Property developer. Wants to pull my café down and put up an office block that will be as big a monstrosity as that." He pointed up at the rollercoaster.

She laughed. "That is one of our biggest attractions."

"It's still brutal."

For the next ten minutes while Joe chattered, Amy negotiated the traffic along the promenade, past the South Pier with its Skyscreamer, reverse bungee ride dominating the skyline, and through the tram junction at Lytham Road, and finally turned right onto Chapel Street near Madame Tussauds, where she pulled into the kerb and parked outside the grey concrete block of the police station.

As they climbed out of the car, Joe looked back to the seafront and the ferris wheel on the Central Pier. The seafront and the pier were packed with day-trippers and holidaymakers.

"Why can't my life be that simple?" he muttered.

"Huh?"

"Nothing. Just having a moan. Come on. Let's see what's what."

Once inside, they found the reception area a scene of chaos, with the Sanford 3rd Age Club members arguing with Vaughan and his associates while Sergeant Ronnie Oldroyd struggled to maintain order. Vaughan, Joe noticed, sported a black eye, and one of the two men with him had a cut lip.

"What the hell is going on?" Joe shouted to make himself heard over the babble.

Comparative silence fell and Oldroyd seemed relieved.

"Are you Joe Murray?"

"Judging by the trouble you're having, I'm tempted to say no.

131

What's happened?"

George Robson stepped forward. "It's summat and nowt, Joe. We were in the Waterloo and this ponce came in hassling Brenda and Sheila." He jerked a thumb at Vaughan. "I told him to back off and he started prodding me in the chest, so I lamped him."

"Common assault," Vaughan snapped.

George clenched his fists. "There's nowt common about the way I assault prats like you, and if you fancy your chances, come on."

Vaughan took half a pace forward, but Oldroyd intervened.

"Just back off," the sergeant warned them.

To ensure George did so, Joe, too, stood between him and Vaughan.

Sheila pointed at Vaughan's associates. "After that, one of those two started on George, so Brenda kicked him."

"Where he won't want to show his mum," Brenda added with an insouciant smile.

"Then Owen got involved and gave the other one a fat lip."

"These men are my personal security officers," Vaughan growled. "They were there to protect me."

"Then you need to get them another job, pal," George snapped. "Try the local primary school."

"All right, all right," Oldroyd insisted. "I've sorted things out as best I can, Mr Murray. Mr Vaughan has registered a complaint against your friends, and Mrs Riley and Mrs Jump have also lodged a complaint against Mr Vaughan for harassment. There was some damage to the pub fittings and furniture, but your friends have paid for that."

"We had a whip round before the paddy wagon turned up," George explained. "Only about a hundred quid."

"The landlord is not pressing charges, and I've warned Mr Vaughan he has to keep his distance from you and your party, and he's given his word," Oldroyd went on.

"Does this have to go any further, Sergeant?" Amy asked.

Oldroyd raised his eyebrows. "And who are you, madam."

"Amy Willows. You know me. I'm the union rep for the drivers at Ballantynes."

"Yes, well, Ms Willows, Ballantynes' influence won't cut any ice on this matter. However, if you, Mr Murray, can vouch for your people, we'll let it go at that."

Joe had known his members too long to cave in that easily. "I'm not their father, you know."

"I'm aware of that, sir, but I'm assured you are the organiser for the Sanford 3rd Age Club."

"And if they start again, I'm the one who gets locked up, am I?"

"Of course not, but it is you'll we'll come to."

Brenda laid seductive eyes on Joe. "We promise to be good little girls and boys."

After some further hesitation, during which, everyone, Sergeant Oldroyd included, looked expectantly at him, Joe resigned himself to the inevitable. "All right. I'll take charge of 'em."

"In that case, sir, they can all go."

"You haven't heard the last of this, Murray," Vaughan warned.

Joe appealed to Oldroyd, who cast a warning glance at the property developer. "Need I remind you, Mr Vaughan, I can still charge you with affray? Now scram. All of you."

Chapter Eleven

From the police station, while George and Owen went off in search of an open pub, Joe and the three women crossed the promenade near Madame Tussaud's and walked onto Central Pier. Shuffling their way through the huge crowds around the funfair, they eventually sat down at a wooden picnic table towards the far end of the pier, and while Sheila, Brenda and Amy tucked into large ice cream cones, Joe settled for a cup of tea and savoured the atmosphere.

As far as he was concerned, it was exactly what a day at the British seaside was all about. The sun shining from a cloudless sky, couples and families ambling along the wooden boardwalk, older people (and a few youngsters) perched on the ornate, cast iron seating along the edge of the pier, excited children, smiling indulgent parents, cash registers at the side stalls ringing with a frequency that made the proprietors smile too, it all spelled carefree; an innocent hedonism that was a far cry from the drudge of the office or factory.

Joe, too, usually obsessed with The Lazy Luncheonette's performance and takings, was glad to be away, to be out and about, his worries left eighty miles behind in the industrial heart of West Yorkshire.

But not entirely.

Two murders at Ballantyne Distribution and Vaughan's antics trying to rack up the pressure were issues he could not escape and they juggled for position at the forefront of his attention.

"You said you'd gone as far as you can with the murders, Joe," Amy pointed out, "and you also told me you'd appealed against the CPO."

"Right on both counts."

"Then forget about them."

"It's not that easy," Joe pleaded. "I'm not stupid. I don't like to be beaten and Vaughan will eventually get his way. The Lazy Luncheonette will be demolished along with the rest of Britannia Parade."

Brenda gulped audibly. Sheila finished her ice cream, and with sharp eyes on Joe, dabbed at her lips with a serviette before challenging him. "You said you'd appealed."

"And so I have, but let's not kid ourselves. I ain't gonna win. The appeal will be rejected and Britannia Parade will be demolished."

"Then what was the point of the appeal?" Brenda demanded.

Before Joe could answer, Amy's mobile bleated out the theme from *The Godfather*. She retrieved it from her bag, checked the menu window, and then opened up a text. Reading it with a puzzled frown, she stood up. "Will you excuse me a moment? I have a call to make."

Joe nodded and watched her shapely behind wander across to the rails where she leaned over and stared across the sea while she dialled.

"Pretty lady," Brenda said.

Her remark brought Joe back to the reality of the picnic table. "Is she? Can't say I've noticed."

Brenda laughed and teased him further. "Course you haven't, Joe. She just reminds you of a classic Stotts Boiler."

Never slow to join in, Sheila commented, "I thought your eyes were going to pop out and roll across the pier after her."

"Can we just leave Amy out of this," Joe grumbled. "You were asking about my appealing the CPO. Well, we have to be realistic. We're not gonna stop the demolition, but that … that … *git*, Vaughan won't let me have a unit in his fancy new block, and that's what I hope I can get from the appeal."

Sheila thought about it. "Considering it'll be an office block,

Joe, even if you did get a unit, we won't get the same passing trade as we do in Britannia Parade."

"Probably not, but the office wallahs will make up some of the difference."

Sheila fell silent for a minute, while Joe studied Amy's behind once more.

"I wonder what the chances are of opening a café in Blackpool," he muttered.

Brenda overheard his remark and responded sarcastically. "That's just what Blackpool needs, isn't it? Another café." Moderating her tone, she went on, "Joe, what does all this mean for our jobs?"

For a moment, he could not look her in the eye. The tracks of his long memory ran over the years they had known each other and worked together. The three-cornered friendship, formed in the schoolyard half a century ago, had endured three marriages, the deaths of their husbands and the departure of his wife, and several years of working as a team. It was founded on the highest principles of honesty and a willingness to help each other without waiting to be asked. He knew that both Sheila and Brenda would fight tooth and nail to save The Lazy Luncheonette, not just because it provided them with employment, but because it was owned and managed by one of their best friends.

That level of support, he decided, warranted complete honesty.

"The truth is, I don't know," he said eventually. "It may be that we can survive as we are. It may be that a job has to go. It may be that we'll need to look at job share." He shook his head, sadly. "I really don't know." Looking up from the table, he cast a fierce glance at them. "I don't want you two worrying about it, either. That's my department."

Brenda smiled. "Okay, Joe. We won't."

Amy concluded her call and ambled back to the table, her brow knitted in either deep concentration or consternation. Joe could not decide which.

She became aware of his eyes on her and smiled as she sat down. "Sorry about that. Union business." Silence fell again and she obviously felt uncomfortable. "Am I, er, intruding on a private conversation."

"No, no," Sheila reassured her. "Like you, we have business worries."

Joe gulped down the last of his coffee. "Tell me something, Amy, how do you go on when the management threaten jobs; people's livelihoods?"

She did not answer immediately. A far-off look in her eyes told Joe she was considering her reply. When she did, he was not surprised by her answer.

"You get realistic," she confessed. "It doesn't happen often at a company like Ballantynes, but when it does, you know that by hook or by crook, management will get their way. We look at natural wastage, first. Those people coming up to retirement who might be persuaded to go early. Then we look at redeployment; finding other work for the employees who may be affected. When we've run out of options, we try to secure the best severance deal we can for those people who will lose their jobs. Is this to do with the murders?"

"No. It's to do with my café. I told you about Vaughan, didn't I? If he gets his way, and he likely will, he could put me out of business, and I have my crew to consider." He pointed alternately at Sheila and Brenda.

Amy put on a pained expression. "I'm sorry. It's the way the world is these days. Money does all the talking."

"It does more than talk," Joe assured her. To change the subject, he nodded at her phone. "Was that concerning Stan and Peter?"

She shook her head. "Different matter entirely. One I have to deal with, though."

Leaving the table, Sheila and Brenda checked a nearby photographic studio specialising in sepia photographs in various period costumes, while Joe and Amy looked over the shoulder of a caricature artist who was working quickly in acrylic inks on a picture of a buxom blonde, exaggerating her already impressive bosom and defining her tiny nose as needle sharp. Giving in to the demands of Sheila and Brenda, all four changed into Victorian garb and posed for a photograph, Joe cast as the patriarch complete with high collar, and fake moustache.

That done, the women then persuaded him to sit for the caricature artist, who highlighted his crinkly hair and increased the size of his ears to turn out someone who looked like *The Simpsons'* character, Moe Syslak. To complete the picture, the artist asked what Joe did for a living, and after inking in a tiny body, he furnished it with a rolling pin and carving knife. Asking for it to be framed, Joe paid for the picture to be sent by post to The Lazy Luncheonette. "I don't wanna carry it around with me. It might get damaged." And with that, they made their way from the pier back onto the promenade.

With time coming up to five, they began the slow walk through the crowds back towards the Monarch, Joe and Amy parting company with Sheila and Brenda at the Coral Island amusement centre, where Amy had left her car in the back street.

As she unlocked the car, and prepared to climb in, Joe said, "Amy, will you have dinner with me, tonight?"

She looked surprised, but also pleased. However, she shook her head. "I'm sorry, Joe, but after that phone call, I have something I need to attend to." Her face brightened. "I could meet you for a drink later."

After his initial disappointment, he perked up. "Great. Where... Hey. Tell you what, why don't you come to the Monarch. There's a disco on at eight. You can meet the rest of the Sanford 3rd Age Club and see them as they really are."

"A bunch of born-again teenagers?" She laughed. "All right. About nine o'clock?"

"I'll be expecting you, so don't let me down."

***

Getting back to his room just before six, Joe showered, and then sat in the window, bringing his notes up to date on the netbook.

Downloading photographs from the depot from his mobile phone, he felt tired, but content. Despite having made what he considered to be little progress at Ballantynes, he had enjoyed the latter part of the afternoon and he was looking forward to seeing Amy again. Vaughan was a problem which could wait until he got back to Sanford. In the meantime, he wanted to enjoy himself.

After an excellent evening meal of cold cuts and house white, dining with Sheila and Brenda, the trio made their way to the bar, where the evening disco, run by a local DJ, soon got under way.

Amy, true to her word, arrived about nine, and Joe spent a short while introducing her to various club members, including Les Tanner, Sylvia Goodson and the Staineses. He was happy to be in her company, and from the off she got on well with Sheila and Brenda, both of whom promised to divulge 'all the dirt on Joe Murray'. The butt of their good-natured humour took it in good part, and with music from the sixties and seventies dominating the evening, he danced with all three at one stage or another.

At ten, during a break in the music, he excused himself and crossed the room to buttonhole Les Tanner, an employee of Sanford Borough Council, on the subject of corruption in the town hall.

"I won't have it, Murray," Tanner declared. "I know Irwin Queenan, and I don't particularly like the fella, but I don't believe he's shifty."

"Then how come he's taking Vaughan's side in this whole

139

affair."

"It's possible that Mr Queenan is just carrying out the wishes of the council," Sylvia said.

"Yes, Sylvia, it is, but it's also possible that Vaughan has dropped him a few thou in order to persuade our elected members to fall in with the redevelopment. I meanersay, there was nothing wrong with Britannia Parade."

"I agree," Tanner said. "There was nothing wrong with it, but it does not project a modern image, and everything in the Town Hall these days is about modernity." Tanner became less formal and more amenable. "Joe, it was old country. If Sanford is to attract new businesses and tackle unemployment, it has to show that it's willing to change. We may not like it, but that's the way it has to be."

"And shut down viable concerns like my café?"

"Small concerns," Tanner corrected. "Yes. It may throw a dozen people out of work, but if it sees hundreds in employment while the new buildings are going up and hundreds more employed when the office block is completed, it's a necessary sacrifice."

***

While Joe debated with Tanner and Sylvia, Amy went to the bar and Brenda took the opportunity to exchange views with Sheila, asking, "What do you think of our Miss Amy?"

Sheila tittered. She had noticed the signs all evening. "I think she is definitely enamoured of our little Joe."

Brenda laughed. "I think so, too. Time for a word to the wise." She stood up.

"Now, Brenda, don't go interfering."

"If I don't, Miss Amy will go home seriously frustrated. I'll be back in a few minutes." Skirting the dance floor, Brenda made for the bar and positioned herself next to Amy. "I thought you might need a lift."

Amy raised an empty tray from the counter. "I'd have managed."

"Yes, well, I'm here now." Brenda mentally rehearsed her opening gambit. "Amy, I hope you don't mind me saying, but I couldn't help noticing you're, er, fond of Joe."

Suspicion clouded Amy's eyes. It needed no reinforcement, but the gravel in her voice stressed it anyway. "Is that any of your business?"

"No. None. But I thought you might appreciate some advice."

The suspicion turned to confrontational anger. "Am I treading on someone's toes, Brenda? Yours for instance? Trying to warn me off?"

Brenda smiled and shook her head. "Nothing like that. Calm down, Amy, or your blood pressure will pop your head off. I'm trying to tell you something about our Joe."

Amy showed no inclination to calm down. "And what's that? He's gay?"

Brenda found the idea amusing and laughed. "No. He's as straight as ... well ... I'm trying to say that he's an idiot."

Brenda pointed behind Amy where the barman was waiting. Amy turned, placed her order, and while the barman prepared the drinks, she faced Brenda again. "What are you talking about? He seems perfectly intelligent to me. And he's good fun when you get him to loosen up."

"I'm not talking about his approach to life in general. Listen, both Sheila and I have known him since our schooldays. He's a clever man. His powers of observation are unequalled. He misses nothing. When it comes to business, he can work profits out in his head while you're still looking for your calculator. He comes across as grumpy and he is a bit outspoken, but he will never see anyone in trouble if he can help. Having said all that, he has this blind spot ... women."

"Women?" Amy had gone from angry to puzzled in too short a time, and she was relieved when the barman tapped her on the shoulder and asked for her money. She paid for the drinks, but instead of picking up the tray, she turned her back to the bar again. "I don't understand."

"He doesn't know how to deal with women. Oh, he has no problem asking for a date. He and I were going steady for a short time in our teens, but he lost out to the man who eventually became my husband. And the reason Joe lost out is because he didn't know how far he was supposed to go at any given point." Brenda sighed wistfully. "Yes, and I wasn't the woman I am now. It wasn't the done thing for a girl to lead the way back then."

"I do remember." Amy sounded slightly less irritated.

"Well, he's still the same. What I'm trying to say is, if you don't take him by the hand, all you're likely to get is a goodnight kiss ... or maybe even a handshake." The enormity of what she had just said struck Brenda. "I'm not insinuating that you're ready to, er ... you know."

"No. Of course not."

"But if you were, you'd have to let him know."

To Brenda's relief, Amy chuckled. "Thank you." She turned to collect her tray. When she turned again, it was to find herself face to face with George Robson and his most alluring smile.

"I'm George. Who are you and aside from the cop shop this afternoon, where have you been all my life?"

"I'm Amy."

"Well, hello, Amy."

She smiled back at him. "Goodbye, George."

He stared at her back as she wriggled her way round the dance floor to join Sheila. "What happened there?"

"Amy has her eyes on bigger fish, George," Brenda explained.

He shook his head. "Not possible. I'm the biggest here, and you know it."

"I'm not talking about your wedding tackle. I mean bigger, richer, smarter and less pushy fish." While George presented a fogged face, she explained, "Joe."

It looked like it had added insult to injury. "Joe? No way is Joe better than me in any department."

Brenda smiled again as she left. "Take it from me, lover boy, Joe is better than you in *every* department."

***

The evening drew to a lively close, with the dance floor still crowded, the bar serving drinks faster than ever and the members of the Sanford 3rd Age Club in party mood.

At their table, while Amy appeared thoughtful and subdued, Joe complained persistently about Les Tanner, Queenan and Vaughan, to the point where Sheila and Brenda took to the floor and he was left with only Amy as an audience.

She deftly changed the subject, asking what he had done with all the notes he had been making at Ballantynes.

He answered as if he believed it should be obvious to her. "Transferred them to my netbook, as usual. And the photographs."

"Photographs of what?" Amy sat bolt upright.

"Peter and Stan," Joe replied diffidently. "It may sound bizarre, but I took pictures of their wounds. That kind of thing can help sometimes."

"But you hadn't been asked to investigate at that time."

He grinned. "No, but I expected to be. Besides, it wouldn't matter if I hadn't been asked. I'd have followed the story in the papers and the moment the cops got it wrong, I would have been shouting."

Amy lapsed into silent contemplation again.

"Something wrong?"

"What? Oh, no. Just thinking. Listen, Joe, do you think I could see these pictures?"

Her suggestion caught him off guard. "They're, er, they're not very pleasant."

"I know that, but … please, Joe. Peter was my husband you

know, and Stan and I … I'd really like to see them."

With a shrug, he finished his beer. "Okay. You sure you can trust me on your own in my room?"

He said it with a grin, and Amy responded with a broad smile.

After a brief word with Sheila, Joe led the way from the bar and up to his first floor room, where he opened the door and let them in.

Inviting her to sit, he dug into the wardrobe and his small suitcase to retrieve the netbook and its mains adaptor.

"It takes a minute or two to boot up," he said from the depths of the wardrobe, "and like I say, the pictures are not pretty."

"Joe, forget the computer."

He stood, turned to face her and to his astonishment found her unbuttoning her blouse.

Throwing it off, she said, "Let me show you something instead."

Chapter Twelve

"Where's your star-crossed lover?" Brenda asked.

Tucking into bacon and eggs, Joe raised his eyebrows. "Who?"

"Amy?"

"Where do you get lover from, never mind star-crossed?"

Brenda tilted a dish forward to scoop out the last of the cereal and milk. "Joe, she was all over you with her eyes last night. Yes, and if I'm not mistaken, she'll have been all over you with more than her eyes later on."

"Jealous, dear?" Sheila asked.

"No, of course not."

"Just nosy," Joe declared, and sliced through the rubbery egg.

"All right, so I'm nosy. Did she spend the night with you?"

Joe shook his head as he ate. Gulping down the piece of egg, washing it down with a mouthful of lukewarm tea, he said, "The hotel would probably have charged me for putting her up. Besides, she lives right here in Blackpool." He smiled at the memory of Amy leaving close on two in the morning. The smile broadened when he recalled the passion before her departure. He caught his two friends looking at him expectantly. "Mind you, she was late getting home. She must have been, the time she left my room."

Brenda was about to dig at Joe for more details when Keith left his table and joined them. "Any news on the bus, Joe?"

"Not so's you'd notice. I'm assured it'll be ready first thing tomorrow morning and they'll bell you when you can go pick it up."

"I bloody hope so."

145

"What's wrong with you, man?" Brenda demanded, venting her irritation on him instead of Joe. "You've had a free weekend in Blackpool, haven't you?"

"It's cost me a bloody fortune, and Her Indoors is on the phone every ten minutes whining cos I'm not home." Keith turned back to Joe. "So how did you get on with those two blokes what killed each other?"

"I didn't get on with it at all," Joe admitted. "And I didn't think you were that interested."

Keith stood up again. "I'm not, but I'll bet he is." He nodded towards the entrance before taking his leave of them.

Joe turned to find Chief Inspector Burrows bearing down on him. He wore the same, faded brown suit he had sported over the last two days, but this time, his appearance was enhanced by a broad smile crossing his face.

Without being invited, he sat between Brenda and Joe and helped himself to a cup of tea. "Just wanted to thank you, Murray."

Finished with the half-warm food, Joe dropped his cutlery onto the plate and drank his tea. Checking the pot, finding it empty, he signalled for a waiter and ordered more before finally turning his attention to the chief inspector.

"Thank me? What for? Dragging this lot out of your bridewell yesterday?" He gestured at Brenda and Sheila.

"Oi," Sheila warned. "We're not 'this lot'."

"I'm not talking about the scuffle in the Waterloo. Think I'd get involved in a battle between a wealthy dipstick, two minders and a mob of middle-aged thugs?"

"And we're not thugs," Brenda said.

"That's true," Joe joked. "They'd rip any self-respecting thug to pieces."

Burrows ignored the banter. "I'm talking about Cruikshank and Crowther."

At the mention of the two men, Joe immediately went on the defensive. "Ah, now I did say to Dave Kane that I'd gone about as far as I could with it. It needs your forensic…" he trailed off as the waiter delivered a fresh pot of tea. When the waiter left again, Joe went on. "It needs your forensic people on it, now."

"Don't be modest, Murray." Burrows' affability made Joe suspicious. "I was persuaded that the two men had killed each other. It was your efforts yesterday which made us aware that they couldn't have done, and that led, indirectly, to this morning's arrest."

Busy pouring more tea for himself Joe almost dropped the pot. "Arrest?"

Burrows nodded slowly and confidently. "Dave Kane."

This time Joe hurriedly put the teapot down to make sure he couldn't drop it. The shock also caused him to raise his voice. "Kane?"

Burrows put a finger to his lips asking for discretion. "Logical when you think about it. He had the opportunity to kill both men. He says he went out to the workshops to check the lorry cab, looking for the flask. Foreman remembers him doing just that, but he can't confirm how long Kane was there. I reckon that from the workshop, he made his way over to the drivers' car park, conned Crowther into moving onto park fifteen and killed him."

Joe took in the information and found he could not safely argue with it. "And Cruikshank?"

"You told me that he came back to security, had a few words with you and your driver, then made an excuse to go into the building. He said he was going to Dispatch, which is on the ground floor. But he admits he also went up to his office on the third floor, and we reckon that's when he hit Cruikshank."

His hands shaking from the revelations, Joe swallowed some tea. "Why did he kill Crowther?"

Burrows answered with a question. "Did Kane tell you he was divorced?"

"Yes. He said he'd been divorced some time."

"About twelve years near as we can make out. Did he also tell you that Crowther was responsible for the divorce? We have it on the best authority." Burrows tapped the side of his nose. "Can't say who told us, but we were pointed straight to Kane. Crowther was fooling around with his wife while Kane was at work."

Joe whistled. "He certainly knows how to put it about, that Crowther."

"Knew how to put it about," Burrows corrected. "He's dead."

Joe ignored the obvious barb. "And Kane's motive for killing Cruikshank?"

"As you suggested. An attempt to frame Cruikshank for killing Crowther. That's what we think, anyway. You did well, Murray, and I'm happy to say I was glad of your input."

"Yes, well, let's not run way with ourselves, eh?" Joe considered everything he had just learned. "Has Kane admitted any of this?"

"Course not. Exactly the opposite. He's denied it all, but we've had him down the nick since six this morning. We're waiting for his lawyer so we can start the interrogation. But trust me, he did it. I'll stake my life on it."

Joe grimaced. "If you've got it wrong, you could certainly be staking your pension on it." Before Burrows could pick him up on the point, he asked, "Do you have any cast iron evidence against him?"

"No, but I'm not worried. I'm sure forensic will turn something up before we're through. That hair you pointed out on the third floor landing was bogus, by the way. It's been there yonks according to our people." Burrows grinned. "What's wrong, Murray? Annoyed that we beat you to it?"

"Of course not. I just said, didn't I, that I'd gone as far as I could. It was up to you and your Scientific Support bods, and if Kane is guilty, then well done." He cradled his cup in his hands. "But there's something that doesn't add up."

"Such as?"

"If I knew that, I'd be telling you, but I don't. It may just be my suspicious mind. What I will say, Burrows, is watch your back. If you openly accuse him and you're wrong, Ballantynes will come down on you like a ton of bricks."

"I'm not a novice, and I know all about Ballantynes. I'll be careful." The chief inspector stood. "Thanks again, Murray. Any time you're in the area, drop in to the station. I'm sure we'll find you a cuppa."

Joe watched Burrows' departing frame. "I'll look forward to it." When he turned back, he found he was the centre of his two friends' attention. "What?"

"You're looking a little put out, Joe," Sheila commiserated.

Brenda was more elliptical. "Who'd have thought it? Tubby Dave Kane a killer."

"It's possible," Joe said, "but unlikely. In fact, I reckon Burrows has it wrong." He settled into his thoughts, poring over mental images and snatches of memory from the previous two days. They came too thick and fast for him to make any sense of them. "I just don't know why."

Sheila chuckled, taking obvious delight from his discomfort. "Come on, Joe, you just told the chief inspector that it's probably your suspicious mind."

"Well, if it is, I'll admit it." He reached into the top pocket of his gilet and took out his mobile. Calling up Amy's number, he dialled. While waiting for the connection, he said, "I just get the feeling that there is something wrong and I need to look into it."

"Oh, Joe," Brenda complained. "We've been here since Friday and we've hardly seen anything of you."

"Goes with the territory when there's a murder," Joe replied. Amy picked up her phone and he concentrated on her. "Amy? Joe. Listen, can you meet me in, say, an hour."

She sounded tired and groggy. "Huh? What? Joe, do you know what time I got to bed last night?"

"About the same time as me, I should imagine. It's vital that we meet. The police have arrested Dave Kane for the killings."

At the other end, Amy was suddenly very alert. "What? That's ridiculous."

"I think so, too, but it is possible. You're the only one who can help me."

There was a moment's silence, disturbed by distant ruffling, which Joe assumed was her throwing off the bed linen. "It's half past nine now. Can you meet me in the Houndshill Shopping Mall in an hour? I'll be at the Coffee House."

"I'll be there."

***

Like any other shopping mall on Easter Sunday, Houndshill was heaving with shoppers when it opened at 10.30 am.

Situated behind the tower, even the approach streets were packed with people enjoying the sunshine, many waiting for the bars to open, others looking for cheap eateries so they could get breakfast out of the way. The short walk along the promenade from the Monarch had revealed that the seafront, too, was thronging. Joe could not recall the last time the Easter weekend had been this hot and sunny, and he felt a great sense of satisfaction for the traders. They were in for a good day.

Wandering through the shopping mall, he ignored the mobile phone and satellite/cable TV salespeople, all eager to attract his attention and draw him into a presentation. Instead, he hurried through the centre to the Coffee House, a small café with pretensions to something grander judging by the smartly attired and fast moving baristas behind the counter. All around him were laminate tables and straight-backed, black, wicker chairs, while the walls were decked with large, monochrome photographs of people drinking coffee. Signs in the backgrounds of some of the images were in Italian, from which Joe assumed the pictures were of Rome.

Amy was already seated near the windows, a latte in front of her. With deliberate emphasis, almost as if he were challenging the place, Joe ordered a pot of tea, paid for it and joined her.

He spent five minutes telling her the tale Burrows had told him. When he was through, he leaned back in his wicker seat, drank his tea and waited for her reply.

When it came, it did not surprise him

"I've never heard such rubbish. Stan Crowther had nothing to do with Dave's divorce."

"You know that for a fact, do you?"

Some of Amy's confidence evaporated. "Well, no, but it's a safe enough bet."

"How so?"

She leaned forward, forearms crossed on the table. "Dave has been divorced well over ten years. At the time, Peter and I were still together, and he used to tell me everything. And remember, he and Stan were good mates. If Stan was involved with Sammy Kane, Peter would have known and he would have told me."

"Sammy?"

"Samantha. Dave's ex."

"Right. I believe you, Amy, but Burrows won't. It's not enough to say it can't be true because you didn't know about it. We need to know who suggested it."

"He's clutching at straws. He wants a quick result and Dave is an obvious target."

Joe smiled and shook his head. "Burrows is a senior officer, not a probationer. Most people have a fairly low opinion of the cops, but I have a niece who's a detective sergeant, and I know for a fact that you don't get to Burrows' rank without using your loaf and watching your back. You need a brain and you need to know when and how to tread carefully. He hasn't just plucked this out of thin air. Someone has pointed him in this direction. He told me so. We need to know who. Now, you know the people at Ballantynes. How many candidates?"

Amy pursed her lips as she considered the question. "Dave's pretty popular, but there are those people who don't like him.

Megan Stafford and Beth Edmunds to name but two."

"I met them. Both in Dispatch?"

"Yes. Traffic managers. They objected to the way Peter was pushed ahead of them as Dave's successor. They both complained to me over it, but as I pointed out, although Peter hadn't worked in the office as long as them, his qualifications were better. They were accusing Dave of sexism, really."

"And you didn't agree?"

"I did … or at least, I suspected it, but Dave had an airtight case. There was nothing I could do other than encourage both women to apply for the job when Dave retires."

"Dave had nothing to do with Megan and Terry Dodd splitting?"

Amy shook her head. "That wasn't an issue for Ballantynes. It was the security contractors who got uppity about it." She sighed. "Joe, I'm saying Beth and Megan were pretty teed off with Dave, but there is no way they would do this to him."

"And Burrows is not likely to tell me who did tip him off." Joe lapsed into silence, his lips pursed, fingers twiddling around his teacup. "I've had this feeling all morning that there's something wrong, something I'm missing, something that's probably staring me in the face, but I'm hanged if I know what."

"Forget about it for a while, then," Amy suggested. "That's what I do. Think about something else, and it'll come to you, so let's do that; talk about something else."

"For example?"

"Your café. Joe, you've told me about your headaches with this development company, but have you ever considered just letting it go and moving somewhere else. Somewhere like Blackpool, for instance?"

He laughed. "I mentioned it yesterday and Brenda said something … or was it Sheila? I can't remember who, but it amounted to Blackpool really needs another café, doesn't it?"

"Look around you. There are never enough cafés here, Joe.

You'll find queues in all of them." Amy's voice took on a new burn of enthusiasm. "I've lived here all my life and I'll say two things about the place: it can give you good, stodgy meals and good drinks. For the traders, it's a licence to print money."

"From Easter to November," Joe pointed out. "But how much trade is there between the end of the illuminations and Easter? Nah, Amy, it's not a bad idea, but it's not for me. I have good, steady trade all year round. Besides, I have my girls to think of, and my nephew."

"Good to hear. But didn't one of them say the developer had offered to pay them off if they persuaded you?"

Joe laughed and finished his tea. "Brenda and Sheila are completely incorruptible. If you offered them the keys to the bank and let them take away all they could carry, they'd turn you down. Me, now I could probably be bought, but it's academic. I said yesterday, didn't I? He will get his way. All I'm doing is angling for a better deal."

"But not cash?"

He shook his head. "People tell me I'm obsessed with money, but I'm not. The business has to make a profit. If it doesn't we go to the wall, but I'm not just a money-grabber. It's more about making him suffer, Vaughan, I mean. Plus I'd like the option for a place in the new buildings."

"And suppose he got really silly and offered you, say, fifty thousand? Surely it would be worth your while?"

Joe laughed. "Pie in the sky. There is no way he would ever offer me that amount of money when all he really has to do is sit back and wait." He stood up. "Come on. Forget about Ballantynes, forget about Vaughan and show me the sights of Blackpool instead."

Amy joined him and they stepped out of the café. "You know the sights of Blackpool. Everyone knows them."

"I mean the *real* sights."

"Ah. The strip clubs and brothels."

Amy laughed and Joe grinned.

They would spend the remainder of the morning and all afternoon together. By silent, mutual consent, their encounter of the previous night was not mentioned. Instead they walked along the promenade as far as the Central Pier, then ducked into the backstreets where they enjoyed a traditional Sunday lunch of roast beef and Yorkshire pudding in a quieter café, before ambling further along the streets until they reached Lytham Road and Hopton Road, where Amy showed Joe the tram sheds, and revealed that she lived just a few doors away.

Joe took the hint and they spent the rest of the afternoon indulging their passion for one another until they both fell into a light, untroubled sleep.

At five, Joe called the police station and spoke to Burrows, only to be told that Kane had singly refused to confess and they were getting short of time.

"We'll either have to charge him or let him go," the chief inspector explained.

With the time coming up to six, they made their way back into the town where Amy picked up her car from Central Drive.

"Fancy another few drinks tonight?" he asked.

"I'm sorry, Joe, I can't," she apologised, but she offered no explanation as to why she could not. "Will I see you tomorrow before you leave?"

He shrugged. "I dunno. Keith has to go to Ballantynes to pick up the bus, so I'm not sure what time we're leaving." He considered his options. "Look, if I don't catch you tomorrow, what say I ring you sometime during the week and make arrangements for us to meet somewhere?"

She laughed. "Neutral territory? Skipton, say?"

Joe grinned by return. "How about it?"

She nodded and kissed him. "All right, Joe. You call and we'll see."

He watched her drive out of the car park, gave her a final wave as she joined the heavy traffic on Central Drive, then began the slow walk back to the Monarch where he would join Sheila and Brenda for dinner and a night in the bar. On the whole, he would rather be elsewhere.

***

It was just after eight when Joe and his friends entered the bar to find the head barman with news for him. "Gentleman over there would like a word, sir." The barman indicated the windows.

Following the pointing finger, Joe was surprised to find Vaughan and his two bodyguards, seated at a window table, looking out across the sea where the sun was dipping rapidly towards the horizon. When he crossed to join them, he discovered the property developer as angry as Joe had ever seen him, and that suited Joe. He, too, was not in the best frame of mind.

He sat opposite the three men. "Don't you understand anything, Vaughan? Didn't the cops warn you to keep your distance? One call to Bonny Street and—"

"I didn't get where I am by running scared of john law, so just shut your mouth and listen for once." Vaughan dragged his malevolent stare from the window to fix Joe in its narrowed field.

Joe refused to be intimidated. "You don't have anything to say that would interest me."

"You don't know until you've heard what I have to say."

The logic was impossible to refute, so Joe shrugged, and Vaughan launched into what sounded like a prepared statement.

"Under the terms of the compulsory purchase order you will receive the market value of your property as it was before redevelopment commenced. Over and above that, you will be paid a substantial sum of money to compensate you for loss of trade during redevelopment."

As Vaughan paused, Joe could not resist commenting. "See, I told you there was nothing I would be interested in. You're telling me what I already know."

"I'm reiterating the situation, and I haven't finished yet," Vaughan argued. After another short pause, he continued, "The new building on the industrial estate is already in place, and—"

"The new *portakabin* on the industrial estate is already in place," Joe interrupted.

Vaughan compromised. "Your new premises are already in place, and they'll be fitted out to your requirements, and all that will not cost you one penny. In short, Murray, all you have to do is pay the rent on that portakabin, which your takings will more than cover. The money you receive from the CPO is yours."

"You're stating the obvious."

"Then here's the unobvious." Again Vaughan paused, this time for emphasis. "I'm willing to pay you fifty thousand pounds. You can have it in cash. The tax man and Sanford Borough Council needn't know about it. It's yours. Put it in your back pocket. Send your two girlfriends and your nephew and his family on a world cruise. Go on one yourself with that union woman from Ballantynes. All you have to do is drop your appeal. And if it makes the deal any sweeter, I'll pay whatever legal expenses you've incurred in setting up the appeal." He sat back. "I can have the money for you first thing tomorrow morning."

The mention of Amy, and the cash offer was too coincidental for it to be a coincidence and Joe found his anger rising. But the object of his fury was not there.

Taking a deep breath, letting it out as a long, slow sigh, he forced himself to relax and searched his innermost feelings. Fifty thousand pounds was tempting, and there was so much he could do with that kind of cash. Move to Blackpool as had been suggested… he preferred not to think about Amy for the moment. She had sold him out. Move to another country, then?

156

Spain, for example. His ex-wife had done it and she had never come back. But it would mean capitulating and mere thought of giving in to Vaughan ignited the anger again.

He controlled the impulse to lash out. Apart from anything else, Appleby and McNeill, the two minders, would probably kick him all round Blackpool. Outspoken he may be, but he had never been built for fighting. Even in the schoolyard, people like Brenda, George and Owen had had to fight his battles for him.

"Fifty grand, eh?" he shook his head and chuckled softly. "You know your trouble, Vaughan? You believe everything has a price tag—"

"Everything does have a price, Murray."

"Yes, but not everything has a *cash* price. I'm not stupid. Somewhere along the line you and Sanford Borough Council are gonna get what you want. I'm determined to make that journey as uncomfortable as possible for you. You can offer me fifty thousand, five hundred thousand, five million, if you want, and the answer will be the same. Stick it. I intend showing the rest of the world, or at least the rest of West Yorkshire, the kind of man you are. You and that crooked little tosspot, Queenan. Keep your filthy money." He threw Vaughan's suggestion back at him. "Take your wife or your mistress, or both on a world cruise, but don't you bother me again, or next time, I really will call the cops."

He got to his feet and marched off to join his friends at the bar.

***

Vaughan looked ready to spit. "That bloody man."

Appleby kept his voice low and neutral. "A couple of phone calls, sir, and I can ensure he never troubles you again."

"Easy enough, to arrange," agreed McNeill.

Vaughan, for all his history of wheeling, dealing persuasion and outright coercion, was appalled. "Are you two out of your minds?"

"No, sir. I just think—"

"I don't pay you to think, Appleby. I pay you to do. And the one thing you don't do is fix it so Murray has an accident. You may think the police are dumb, but they're not. If anything happens to Murray they'll soon put it all together and come knocking on my door. No. Murray, his two whores and his gormless nephew are bulletproof, and he knows it." Vaughan's anger began to boil over. "But there's more than one way to deal with the little snot." He drained his glass and stood. "Come on. Let's get back to the hotel. I need to speak to some people."

***

Across the room Joe, Sheila and Brenda watched them leave.

"So what did he offer, Joe?" Brenda asked. "The stick or the carrot?"

Joe swallowed a mouthful of lager. "Carrot. Fifty thousand in cash, tax free and all I have to do is drop my appeal."

Brenda gaped but Sheila was more piteous. "Oh, Joe, why didn't you take it?"

Coming from her, it was the kind of statement which would usually cause Joe's eyebrows to shoot up, but he had an idea where she was going. He merely waited until she carried on.

"You said yesterday that you're going to lose eventually. You could have taken the money and really profited from it."

"The way you didn't take the ten thou' he offered you?"

"The Lazy Luncheonette is not our business, Joe," Brenda said, obviously picking up on Sheila's track. "And we have no more power to persuade you than anyone else."

"Fifty grand is peanuts to him. He's probably lost twice that this last week. And I have you to think about you two, and Lee. And even if it's not exactly peanuts to me, I don't need the money."

"First, you don't have to worry about Brenda and me," Sheila said, "and second, even if you don't need the money, you could have used it to set Lee up in his own business."

"He has his own business," Joe pointed out. "The Lazy Luncheonette. It's his when I shuffle off. Besides, if I wanted to set the lad up, I'd rather do it with clean money. My money." Emptying his glass, he signalled the barman for refills. "Interesting offer, though. It told me just what a mug I've been again."

"Mug?" Brenda asked.

"Amy. She set me up." He went on to tell them of the exchange in the Coffee House earlier in the day.

"Oh, Joe, I'm so sorry," Brenda sympathised.

"Yeah, me too. I really liked her, you know. Still, what else am I good for if not for some woman to take advantage of?" He picked up his beer. "Come on. There's another disco in here shortly. Let's boogie the night away, eh?"

Chapter Thirteen

Despite the Monday morning sunshine and the promise of another hot day, a great depression had settled on Joe. He had had precious little sleep, thanks to the twin problems of Ballantyne Distribution's killings and Amy's treason churning over and over in his head. Eventually, things reached a point where his frustration turned to anger, and that only exacerbated his insomnia.

At breakfast, while Brenda and Sheila chattered garrulously, reflecting on how they had enjoyed their weekend, he was sleepy, surly and uncommunicative, brooding over his cereal and bacon and eggs.

"We're sorry about Amy," Sheila told him when they eventually broached the matter. "And we're sorry about the work you've done on those murders, but it's the police's problem not yours."

"Theirs and Dave Kane's," Brenda agreed. "And if you're right, if he really is innocent, they'll get there. You've always said the police are good at what they do, but they're just not as quick as you."

"Forget Amy," Joe growled. "She's history, but Dave Kane … what am I supposed to do? Leave him to rot in a cell for a crime I'm sure he didn't commit? I've had some of that, remember. Valentine's last year. It's not pleasant. In fact, it's all wrong, and I can prove it. I know I can." He fell silent again. "I just don't know how."

As if sensing the time was right to cut in on the argument, Keith came over to them. "I've had the call from Ballantynes, Joe. I'm getting a taxi over there now. I've the bus to check and sign for, and I should be back here for about half ten. So if you can have your people out of here and ready for loading."

"Yeah, right, Keith. Spread the word as you leave, eh?"

"Will do."

Joe and his companions stood and made their way from the dining room.

"Have you much packing to do, Joe?"

"Only the netbook," he promised. "I'll be five minutes."

While they waited for the lift, Sheila asked, "Getting back to Dave Kane, what makes you so sure he's innocent? Is it because Amy said so?"

"I told you to forget Amy, didn't I?" Joe retorted. "All right, she does know him better than me, but after what she did to me, do I really care what she has to say? It's just… I dunno… He's not the murdering type."

"That's opinion, not evidence," Brenda said. "And you always say opinion doesn't count."

"It doesn't."

"Good," Brenda said. "Because, if you want *my* opinion, Kane looks like Humpty Dumpty."

Sheila tittered as the lift doors opened. "Except that he isn't tall enough to get on the wall."

Joe tutted and pressed the button for the first floor. "Get personal, why don't you? As if the poor bugger hasn't enough to put up with, now you're insinuating he's a dwarf."

"And you know what that feels like, don't you, Joe?"

The lift rose quickly, came to a stop and the doors soughed open, Brenda delivered a cheeky grin and followed Sheila out.

"I'll see you in a few minutes," Joe said and cut into his room.

Once there, he tossed his netbook into the case, zipped it up, then stood for a few moments at the window, looking out on the North Pier and the War Memorial, The Exchequer across the square, and the early holidaymakers out enjoying the spring sunshine. He had had just one afternoon of such enjoyment, and now he regretted it. He should have refused to help Ballantynes, and spent the weekend with his friends. If nothing else, it would have saved him the hurt and anger he felt at Amy's betrayal.

It was too late now. First thing tomorrow morning, he would be back behind the counter of The Lazy Luncheonette, doubling up in the kitchen, helping Lee get the meals out, feeding the ever-hungry stomachs of the draymen and factory hands, or stretching over hot gas rings to reach the top pie racks, and…

His thoughts came to a tumbling halt.

He looks like Humpty Dumpty.

Except that he isn't tall enough to get on the wall.

Why don't they position these shelves for someone who's only five foot three?

Joe's heart began to pound. It was so obvious when he thought about it, but like everyone else, he hadn't thought about it. It may not point the finger at the real culprit, but it would surely save Kane's hide.

He dug into the suitcase, took out his netbook again, removed it from its case, opened it up and switched on, silently willing it to hurry through its boot routine. While he waited, he made a last check of the room, ensuring that he had not left anything behind. By the time he was happy that he had all his belongings, the netbook was running and waiting for his input. He opened up the photograph album and checked the pictures he had taken. Yes. There it was. No doubt about it.

His phone rang. He checked the menu. Lee. He made the connection.

"Uncle Joe—"

"Not now, Lee. I'm up to me neck in it. I'll call you later."

Closing off the phone, shutting down the machine again, he tucked the netbook in its own case and, dragging his small suitcase behind him, left the room and hurried along the corridor to Sheila and Brenda's door where he knocked and waited, his foot tapping impatiently on the carpet.

Brenda opened the door.

"Listen, I've just got it. I can prove that Dave Kane is innocent. Can you look after my luggage while I get over there? Tell Keith to pick me up at the police…" Joe trailed off, his attention taken by the view of the sea from their window. "I thought you said you had a cracking view from here."

"We do," Brenda said as he walked in. "We can see the sea."

"What use is that? You've seen water before, haven't you? You told me you could see the Central Pier and the Pleasure Beach."

"You can," Sheila pointed to the right hand side of the windows. "If you stand there and press your face to the window, you can just make out The Big One, and you can see Central Pier sticking out in the water."

Joe did as she said and was rewarded with the tiny glimpse of both landmarks.

"You need to be in the right place to see it, Joe," Brenda told him.

Once more his heart began to palpate. "Oh my God. That's it."

They had seen this kind of performance so often that the glances passing between Sheila and Brenda were anything but surprised.

"What's it, Joe?" Sheila asked, softly.

"The answer. It's so simple I can't believe I've wasted all weekend trying to crack it."

"Yes, you've already said you can prove Dave Kane innocent," Brenda reminded him.

"I can do more than that," he told them as he dug into his gilet, searching for his phone. "I can tell Burrows who did it." With the chief inspector's business card in front of him, he tapped out the numbers with shaking fingers and put the phone to his ear. "Do me a favour," he said while he waited to be connected. "Load my case onto the bus and get Keith to pick me up—"

"At the police station. We know."

"No. Not at the police station. I'll be at Ballantyne Distribution."

"What?"

"Where?"

"Chief Inspector Burrows."

At the announcement, Joe ignored his friends and concentrated on the phone call. "Burrows, it's Joe Murray. Listen to me. If you still have Dave Kane in custody, you have the wrong man, and I can prove it. Better than that, I can tell you who really did it. I'm on my way to Ballantynes now. Bring Dave and enough people to make the arrest."

"Now listen, Murray—"

"I mean it. Dave Kane is not guilty, but I know who is."

***

By the time Joe got to Ballantynes, he had already spoken to Amy. He had been curt with her, but insistent that she get in touch with Megan and ask her to be there too.

"Why Megan?" Amy had asked.

"Because she knows more than she's ever let on," Joe replied.

At the gatehouse, he was signed in by Terry Dodd. "Listen, Terry, can you spare a few minutes to be in the Dispatch office?" Joe asked as he slipped on the borrowed hi-vis vest.

"Why?"

"Because I need to show the cops something, and you're the only one I know who's tall enough." Joe smiled encouragingly. "Plus, I have a feeling the killer may try to do a runner when he's confronted."

"You know who it is?" Dodd still did not sound interested.

"I think I do, but I may need your help."

Dodd sniffed disinterestedly. "I'll be there."

The next obstacle was Sandra Hamilton who refused to even show him Friday's security log, let alone print off a copy for him.

"It can prove one way or another who's guilty," Joe insisted.

"I don't care if it can prove the Earth is flat," she retorted. "I caved in on Saturday, but not again."

"We'll have to see what Burrows says about it," Joe said as Terry Dodd joined them.

"He can say what he likes. Without a warrant, he gets nothing," Sandra snapped, and then glowered at Dodd. "And what do you want?"

"He's helping me," Joe explained. "Thanks, Terry. I'll see you in Dispatch in a few minutes."

Amy and Megan were next to arrive while Joe continued to press Sandra for the security log. He was surprised to see Amy there, and said so.

"Megan is one of my members. I want to know what's going on," she explained.

He asked them to go to Dispatch and wait for him, then returned to his negotiations.

"I said no, I meant no," Sandra replied.

"Are you always this difficult?"

"You should see me on a blind date," she said.

It was only when Chief Inspector Burrows and two of his CID officers showed up that she finally capitulated.

Kane was with them. A night in police custody had done him no favours. He was red-eyed, unshaven, unkempt, and he had a haunted, troubled look about him which spoke of worries more serious than running a logistics operation.

Directing the two officers and Kane to the Dispatch office, Joe explained the situation to Burrows, who turned on Sandra and insisted on seeing the security log.

"It's more than my job is worth," she told the chief inspector.

"It'll be more than your freedom is worth, lass," Burrows told her. "Now either do it, or I run you in for obstructing a police officer in the course of his duties."

She continued to carp, but Joe could see her resolve

165

crumbling, and eventually, she gave way.

When the log appeared on screen, Joe checked it, and his face broke into a broad grin. "See." He pointed out the two key entries to Burrows. "There's your answer: the real killer."

Burrows checked the screen and was satisfied. "All right, Murray. It's your show. Print that out for us, please," he said to Sandra.

"But—"

"Now listen, this is a murder investigation, not a search for a missing box of paperclips. Just get it printed out."

A few minutes later, armed with the printouts, Joe and Burrows made their way through the noisy Sort Centre, and into Dispatch. The two policemen had stationed themselves by the counter to move inquisitive drivers on. Dodd was by the main door, while Amy, Megan and Kane stood by the back wall, chatting quietly.

"Sorry to keep you waiting," Joe apologised as he plugged in his netbook and switched it on. "One of the problems with this investigation has been the nitpicking of your security people… no offence, Terry."

"No worries. It gets on my wick, too."

"We've just come up against it again, but, it's all sorted and we have everything we need now." Joe paused a moment, marshalling his thoughts. "You know, I have two very good friends: Sheila Riley and Brenda Jump. Whenever I'm stuck on an investigation, I can almost guarantee that they'll say something which will tip the scales, and they did exactly that this morning." Looking around, he crossed to a desk and picked up a twelve-inch ruler. "A couple of days ago, I took photographs of the injuries of both men. Other people thought it was weird, but that kind of thing can often help in a case like this. It's the very reason the police take photographs at crime scenes. Now, although I didn't realise it at the time, those pictures actually told me something about the killer, and this morning, after a remark from Sheila, they told me that Dave

Kane could not have killed either man. He's not tall enough."

Amy chuckled, Megan looked shocked and Kane scowled. "Thanks a lot, Joe."

Ignoring him, Joe went on. "Let me show you." He smiled encouragingly at Dodd. "Can I borrow you for a minute, Terry?"

With a disinterested shrug, Dodd ambled to the centre of the room. "Let's imagine I was going to strike Terry in the same way Stan and Peter were struck." With the ruler playing the role of the murder weapon, he stretched out his arm, and laid the straight edge across Dodd's neck at an angle, running up from the shoulder to the far side of the neck. "You see that? If I were to hit Terry with a truncheon or something like that, the bruise would be at an angle. It's because Terry is taller than me. I have to reach up." He called up the photographs he had taken of Crowther and Cruikshank, and ranged them side by side on the netbook's small screen. The photographs I took showed me that the bruise on Peter's neck wasn't at an angle, and neither was it on Stan's."

"Wrong," Burrows interjected. "One of the wounds on Crowther's neck was angled from shoulder upwards."

Joe brought the image of Crowther to the fore. "The top wound, yes," he said, pointing it out with the ruler. "But the chances are that Stan would have been either flat on the ground or at least on his knees when that was delivered. The primary injury, the first blow, which he would have suffered while he was standing, is straight across, not angled." Again he pointed out the lower injury running across the back of Stan's neck parallel to his shoulders.

Burrows shrugged. "Okay. I'll go with that."

"It all means that the killer was at least as tall as Peter and Stan. Amy, you knew them both well. How tall were they?"

She shrugged. "I don't know. Six feet, maybe a little over or under."

"And, Dave, you're five feet three. Am I right?"

Kane ran a hand over his stubbly chin. "You don't have to rub it in."

"I'm actually saving your arse, pal," Joe insisted and then spoke to the rest of the room. "If Dave had struck either man, we would have seen a different pattern of bruising. Angled from one shoulder or the other to the base of the skull. As far as I'm concerned then, Dave did not kill them. He'd have to stand on a box to deliver those blows because he simply isn't tall enough."

"So who did kill them?" Kane asked.

"I'm just coming to that," Joe replied. His mobile bleated and he let out a soft curse. Taking it from his pocket he read the menu window and made the connection.

"Uncle Joe—"

"I've told you once, Lee, I'm busy. I'll call you back later."

"But, Uncle Joe—"

"I said I'll call you back." Joe cut the connection and smiled apologetically at his audience. "Sorry about that. Nearly thirty years old, and he still can't make decisions for himself." He put the phone back in his pocket. "Now, where was I?"

"You were going to tell us who killed Crowther and Cruikshank," Burrows reminded him.

"So I was. I worked it out this morning, and again, I have to thank my two friends for the tip off. Not that they actually knew they were tipping me off. They were just wittering."

"So are you," Dodd said.

"Yeah, I am, aren't I?" Joe laughed. "The key to it all goes back to something that happened on Friday and other information which Dave gave me on Saturday. Something the view from Brenda and Sheila's room reminded me of. Y'see, on Friday, while Keith, our bus driver, and I were talking to Dave in reception, a team of security men came galloping through. They were on their way to Maintenance where the apprentices were using the wheelie bins for chariot racing. To me it was just one of those crackpot things you hear about in large companies like this. But on Saturday, Dave told me that because of its

168

location, the workshops, and particularly the workshop yard, can only be seen from two places on the entire site. You can't even see it from ground level because other buildings block the view. The only place it can be seen is from the windows in Dave's office and those on the third floor staircase landing." Joe stared around the room, ensuring they were hanging on his words. "One of the guards said the report had only just come through. Which means that the incident was reported from the third floor at about the time Peter Cruikshank was fighting for his life. We know that Peter was on the third floor not long before he died, and it's a safe bet that whoever reported it also killed Peter. And if he killed Peter, then he also killed Stan." Joe spun on his heels and faced his adversary. "Didn't you, Terry?"

Although the announcement was greeted with gasps from the room, Dodd did not appear in the least put out. "You're losing the plot, pal."

"No," Joe replied. "I only just gathered the plot. When I asked on Saturday, you told me you didn't go the third floor. You said you were using one of the rest rooms in the Sort Centre."

"It's the truth."

Joe held up the security log. "Then how come you reported the apprentices fooling around?" He turned the paper towards himself and read from it. "Two fifty-nine. Report from Officer T. Dodd, safety issue, Maintenance Workshops." Joe glared defiantly. "The only way you could have seen them was from the third floor."

Dodd maintained his insouciant nonchalance. "All right, so I was up there. Don't mean I killed Cruikshank ... or Crowther."

"But you did. You tampered with Stan's flask and got him drunk—"

"When?" Dodd demanded. "Check the duty roster. You'll find I was on the gate all morning."

"Yes, and that's when you did it." Joe held up the security log again. "Oh seven ten, cab search, Officer T. Dodd, driver S.

Crowther. Stan would have been out of his cab and you slipped a good dose of absinthe into his flask while you were supposed to be searching it. He even complained to Dave Kane, Amy and Peter Cruikshank later in the day concerning the hold up." Joe tossed the log sheet on the desk. "You got him drunk in the hope that he'd wipe himself out on the motorway, but when he got back, you knew you were in trouble. Dave asked you to move the truck, and you took the opportunity to steal the flask this time, and probably hid it in the gatehouse until you were ready to come to the Sort Centre for your break. Meantime, you waited for Stan to leave the building, cut across the yard to park fifteen and when he got to his car you called him. He came to the rear of the trailer, and you hit him twice. Once to put him down, a second time to make sure he was dead. Then you made your way into the building via the front entrance so no one would suspect you and went up to the third floor where you were busy planting the flask in Peter's locker when he came in and caught you, so you hit him, too. But that locker room is a bit more public than park fifteen, so you couldn't risk hanging around to clout him a second time. Instead, you made your way over to the staircase, and spotted the apprentices playing silly buggers in the workshop yard. Perfect for you, because if anyone asked, you were on legitimate business up there, spying on the apprentices."

From behind, Burrows intervened. "Hang on, Murray. Just what is he supposed to have used as a weapon?"

"His flashlight," Joe said pointing at the instrument hanging from Dodd's belt. "If you check it, you'll see it's a heavy duty thing. Uses three or four batteries. And the body of that torch has the same cross-hatch pattern as the bruises showed. You may have to check every torch in the security stores, but you'll find traces on one of them. Traces of him, too, I hope."

Dodd affected further disinterest with a fake yawn. "Shoot your mouth off, pal. You can't prove one word of this."

"I think I can." Joe addressed the whole room again. "His

antics with women made Stan Crowther a troublemaker. Some years ago, he reported Dodd and Megan, here. Probably because he fancied his chances with Megan. Dodd chose to drop her because he liked his job here, but it still rankled. When Stan came back in one piece on Friday, drunk but having survived, Dodd knew how to deal with it, but the timing had to be right. He needed to know when Stan would be leaving the site so he could intercept him from park fifteen. So he asked you, Megan, to call him, didn't he?"

She did not speak but began to blush furiously.

"And when it became obvious, yesterday, that the police were looking for a single killer, he rang you again, didn't he? This time he asked you to help pin it on Dave." Joe's eye burned into her. "Talk to me, Megan."

Tears welled in her eyes, and she suddenly broke down. "I didn't know he was going to kill Stan. He just said he was gonna rub it in that Stan had been fired. Then when Peter was killed, I was in a panic."

"And that's why you were crying in the rest room, isn't it?"

She nodded frantically. "I was scared. Then later, he told me to fit Dave up or he'd see to me, too. I was more than scared. I was terrified." She turned to face Kane. "I'm sorry, Dave. I didn't want to do it, but…"

Kane glowered at her. He appeared ready to attack her, but before he could move, and with a speed that took everyone by surprise, Dodd pushed Joe to floor and bolted for the exit.

The two police officers were slow to react, but kicked their heels in pursuit. Picking himself up, Joe joined everyone else at the door to the Sort Centre, in time to see Dodd crash into a pallet of flatpack furniture where he was caught and pinned down by the two policemen.

Joe smiled triumphantly. "See. I said the killer would try to do a runner."

Chapter Fourteen

Joe and Amy followed the police from Dispatch through the Sort Centre. Up ahead, Dodd was handcuffed between the two CID men, and behind them, Megan walked alongside Burrows.

Kane had been effusively grateful to Joe, shaking his hand vigorously and promising the moon and sixpence. His joy turned to a scowl of utter contempt when Burrows cautioned Megan but declined to handcuff her.

"What'll happen to her?" Amy asked as they passed through security and emerged into the bright sunshine.

"Withholding evidence. It's a serious crime … or it can be. Burrows isn't a bad old stick and she was under duress. As long as she co-operates and is willing to testify she'll probably get away with a suspended sentence, maybe even probation." Joe kept his tones neutral. Soon he would have to confront Amy, but for now, he was happy to indulge in small talk. "What will Ballantynes do with her?"

"She'll have a criminal record, Joe. It's one of the few things you can be fired for." She chewed her lip. "As her union rep, however, I have to fight her corner and I do feel sorry for her. Terry Dodd has always been an arrogant bully, and that should count for something in her favour. I'll try persuading Dave to redeploy her. After what she's done, he won't want her working in our department, but she's a capable administrator. There'll be other areas, other departments which can use her."

The police vehicles pulled away, making for the main gate. They crossed the roadway and followed the pedestrian footpath in the same direction.

"Your bus is waiting." Amy pointed beyond the gates where

the STAC coach stood, Keith leaning against the rear of the vehicle, glancing occasionally at his watch.

"He's eager to get home," Joe said. "Misses his wife, I think."

"And what about you?" Amy asked as they neared the gatehouse. "Are you in a hurry to get home?"

"Nope, but I have to be there to open up tomorrow morning. I'm self-employed, remember. If I don't do it, no one does."

"But you left it for a whole weekend." Amy moved closer to him. "Couldn't someone else deal with it? You could stay on for a couple of days. Catch up on the enjoyment you missed."

Joe did not answer immediately. Her nearness tempted him, but he could still taste the bile of her actions. He looked first at the coach, then at the Sort Centre, and finally at Blackpool Tower, striking into the cloudless sky. He fixed her eyes with his gaze. "I know, Amy."

She feigned puzzlement. "Know? Know what?"

"You couldn't join us for dinner on Saturday evening. You turned up later, slept with me, and again on Sunday, but only after you'd shown some interest in what it would take to get me to let go of The Lazy Luncheonette. Vaughan got to you, didn't he? He was the one you rang when we were on Central Pier."

She sighed. "Joe—"

"No point trying to deny it. He came up with exactly the offer you'd hinted at in the Coffee House. Fifty thousand pounds. How much did he offer you to get me to give in?"

Another sigh. "Ten thousand. In cash."

Joe's wan smile hardly faded.

"Do you want to hear the rest of it?" Amy's face was lined with pain.

He shook his head.

"I'm going to tell you anyway," she said. "I told him where he could shove his money."

Shock ran through Joe. "What?"

"When we were on Central pier on Saturday, the text I

received was from my boss. Vaughan overheard my name and where I worked when I was talking to Sergeant Oldroyd at the police station. He rang my boss asking for my number. He didn't get it, of course, but the boss promised to talk to me and ask me to ring Vaughan back. He texted me, I rang Vaughan and we met. But I'm a union woman, Joe. People are my business, not profits. I could see how much your café meant to you. When I got into bed with you, it was because I wanted to and not because that rich idiot paid me to. When I suggested you move to Blackpool, it's because I wanted to see more of you." She let out a frustrated sigh. "You obviously weren't joking when you mentioned your suspicious mind the other day."

Joe did not believe her. He ran through the events in his mind. "You said you couldn't see me last night. You knew Vaughan would be at the Monarch, didn't you? And you didn't want to be there in case it turned nasty."

Amy looked away. When she looked back the pain was even deeper. "I told you, I had other matters to deal with."

His tone of voice left no doubt of his scepticism. "Such as?"

"Children, Joe. A grown up son and daughter. In case it's escaped your attention, their father was murdered on Friday. I may not have loved Peter anymore, but they did, and last night they needed their mother."

Joe was mortified. His mind hammered the question at him. How could he have misjudged her so badly?

His wrinkled brow creased even further. "I ... er ... look ... Amy ... oh, sh ... sugar. How the hell have I got into this mess? I'm sorry. I really thought... For God's sake, I wish Vaughan were here right now. I'd throttle him." He sucked in his breath. "I am truly sorry. Is there anything I can do to make amends?"

She took a long time, but eventually, she made her decision and faced him again. "You could make sure I do see more of you."

"Even though I just shot myself down in flames?"

"According to Brenda, you're good at that, especially when it comes to reading women."

Joe leaned into her and kissed her cheek. "Sanford is eighty miles from Blackpool. Let's see how things pan out." He glanced over at Keith, who was checking his watch again and tapping his feet impatiently on the ground. "In the meantime, kiddo, I'd better get a move on."

"Call me," she said as he walked quickly away.

He turned to face her and carried on walking backwards. "Count on it."

Amy stood at the gatehouse and watched him all the way to the coach where an irritable Keith harangued him.

"About bloody time. It was like watching *Casablanca*." He mimicked a woman's voice. "If you're not on that bus, Joe, you'll regret it."

"Just shut it and let's get moving."

Keith climbed aboard, Joe turned and waved one last time to Amy. As he was about to step onto the bus, a familiar figure rushed up to him.

"Hello, Mr Murray."

He studied the woman and searched his memory. "Paula, isn't it? Paula Guy. Did they mend your car for you?"

"Oh, yes. Done a smashing job on it, too." She waved at her car fifty yards along the road. "I saw your bus and I just wanted to thank you for helping us out on Friday."

"No problem, luv. Have you had a good weekend?"

"Brilliant. The kids loved every minute of it. What about you?"

Joe smiled thinly. "It's been interesting."

With a final wave, Paula hurried off to her car and Joe climbed on the bus to a muted cheer from his members.

"At last," Keith complained as he operated the lever to close the door. He engaged the automatic transmission, released the parking brake, and with a check on the mirrors pulled away.

Stowing his netbook on the overhead luggage rack above

Sheila, Joe settled into the jump seat, and ignoring the safety belt, half turned to face his two closest friends.

"So, everything's sorted, Joe?" Brenda asked.

"It's been a bad weekend," he said. "In fact, I haven't had a weekend."

"You will get involved in these things." Brenda smiled to show she was only joking.

Sheila was more generous. "You saved an innocent man from possible proceedings, and you helped jail a killer, Joe." She, too, smiled. "We saw the police cars carrying him away."

"And you look like you've just kissed and made up with Amy," Brenda said.

"Ten out of ten for observation," Joe applauded. "The trouble is I didn't do anything about the problems we have back home, and I didn't get much in the way of enjoyment, did I?"

"We saw Vaughan off," Brenda said with a twinkle in her eye. "And I'm willing to bet you enjoyed Amy."

Joe's phone bleated for attention. "Vaughan will be waiting for us in Sanford," he said taking out the phone and reading the menu. "And as for Amy, you can mind your own business." He made the connection and put the phone to his ear.

"Uncle Joe?"

"Lee? You've been pestering me all morning. What the hell do you want, boy?"

Lee's voice sounded shaky and scared. "It's The Lazy Luncheonette, Uncle Joe."

"What about it?"

"It's burned down."

THE END

Fantastic Books
Great Authors

Meet our authors and discover our exciting range:

- Gripping Thrillers
- Cosy Mysteries
- Romantic Chick-Lit
- Fascinating Historicals
- Exciting Fantasy
- Young Adult and Children's Adventures

Visit us at:
www.crookedcatpublishing.com

Join us on facebook:
www.facebook.com/crookedcatpublishing

Lightning Source UK Ltd.
Milton Keynes UK
UKOW04f1856260116

267187UK00001B/10/P

9 781909 84160